James Hadley Chase and The Murder Room

››› This title is part of The Murder Room, our series dedicated to making available out-of-print or hard-to-find titles by classic crime writers.

Crime fiction has always held up a mirror to society. The Victorians were fascinated by sensational murder and the emerging science of detection; now we are obsessed with the forensic detail of violent death. And no other genre has so captivated and enthralled readers.

Vast troves of classic crime writing have for a long time been unavailable to all but the most dedicated frequenters of second-hand bookshops. The advent of digital publishing means that we are now able to bring you the backlists of a huge range of titles by classic and contemporary crime writers, some of which have been out of print for decades.

From the genteel amateur private eyes of the Golden Age and the femmes fatales of pulp fiction, to the morally ambiguous hard-boiled detectives of mid twentieth-century America and their descendants who walk our twenty-first century streets, The Murder Room has it all. **›››**

The Murder Room
Where Criminal Minds Meet

themurderroom.com

James Hadley Chase (1906–1985)

Born René Brabazon Raymond in London, the son of a British colonel in the Indian Army, James Hadley Chase was educated at King's School in Rochester, Kent, and left home at the age of 18. He initially worked in book sales until, inspired by the rise of gangster culture during the Depression and by reading James M. Cain's *The Postman Always Rings Twice*, he wrote his first novel, *No Orchids for Miss Blandish*. Despite the American setting of many of his novels, Chase (like Peter Cheyney, another hugely successful British noir writer) never lived there, writing with the aid of maps and a slang dictionary. He had phenomenal success with the novel, which continued unabated throughout his entire career, spanning 45 years and nearly 90 novels. His work was published in dozens of languages and over thirty titles were adapted for film. He served in the RAF during World War II, where he also edited the RAF Journal. In 1956 he moved to France with his wife and son; they later moved to Switzerland, where Chase lived until his death in 1985.

By James Hadley Chase
(published in The Murder Room)

Hand Me a Fig-Leaf

James Hadley Chase

An Orion book

Copyright © Hervey Raymond 1981

The right of James Hadley Chase to be identified as the author of this work has
been asserted in accordance with the Copyright, Designs and Patents Act 1988.

This edition published by
The Orion Publishing Group Ltd
Orion House
5 Upper St Martin's Lane
London WC2H 9EA

An Hachette UK company
A CIP catalogue record for this book is available from the British Library

ISBN 978 1 4719 0408 0

www.orionbooks.co.uk

1

The intercom buzzed.

Chick Barley, who was having his second drink of the morning, slopped some Scotch from his glass, cursed, then thumbed down the switch.

Glenda Kerry's voice came out of the box in a loud and metallic squawk.

"Dirk to the Colonel, and pronto!" she snapped and cut the connection.

Chick looked over at me at my desk.

"You heard the lady. The trouble with that chick is she isn't getting it regularly. When a chick doesn't ..."

But I was on my way, pounding down the long corridor to Colonel Victor Parnell's office.

I had been with the Parnell Detective Agency for exactly a week. The agency, the best and most expensive on the Atlantic coast, was located on the top floor of the Truman building on Paradise Avenue, Paradise City, Florida. The agency catered for the rich and the plush and I was still in awe of the luxury atmosphere the set-up exuded.

Colonel Parnell, a veteran of the Vietnam war, with money inherited from his father, had set up the agency some five years ago and had made an instant success. He employed twenty operators, most of them ex-cops or ex-military policemen who worked in pairs. I was a replacement and was lucky to be paired with Chick Barley, a massively built, sandy-haired ex-military police lieutenant, regarded as Parnell's best operator.

I was lucky to have got the job as the competition was fierce. I only got it because my father, in the past, had done Parnell a favour. I never knew just what he did do for Parnell, but the colonel wasn't a man to forget.

For the past thirty years, my father had run the *Wallace Investigators' Service* in Miami, specializing in divorce work. After I had gone through college, I joined the firm, and for ten years had worked as an investigator. My father had taught me all he knew, which was plenty, but finally old age caught up with him and he decided to retire. By then the agency was way downhill. At one time, he had employed three operators, plus me. By the time he decided to retire, I was the only operator and had little or nothing to do.

Colonel Parnell was looking for a replacement for one of his operators who had turned crooked.* My father wrote to him, suggesting he could do worse than employ me. The interview went well and now I was working for the Parnell Agency, a big step up from the defunct agency my father ran, and which he closed down when I left for Paradise City.

As a new boy, I had had a week, working with Chick on a self-service store theft. It had been a dull assignment, but most operators expect dull assignments: either wife-watching or husband-watching or trying to trace missing people and what have you. To be a successful operator you have to have patience, toughness and an inquiring mind. I had all these, plus ambition.

Parnell worked closely with the Paradise City police. If there was any suspicion that the assignment he was given was criminal, he would alert Chief of Police Terrel.

*See *A Can of Worms*

Working this way, he had full co-operation with the police and, for an operator, this was important.

There were other much more important assignments with the rich that the police knew nothing about: blackmail, daughters running off with no-gooders, drunken wives, homosexual sons and so on: assignments kept secret and here Parnell made big money. The rich came to him and revealed, in confidence, the skeletons in their cupboards. I had heard about this from Chick. Sooner or later, he told me, I would be promoted to the upper echelon to help the rich cover up their murky problems.

I tapped on Parnell's door, waited a moment, then walked into the spacious, comfortably furnished office, so unlike the dark, gloomy little room from which my father operated.

Parnell was looking out of the big window that gave onto Paradise Avenue, the sea and the miles of beach. He turned.

Parnell was a giant of a man, on the wrong side of sixty. His fleshy sun-tanned face, small piercing blue eyes and the rat-trap of a mouth stamped him as a veteran soldier, and don't-let-us-forget-it.

"Come in, Dirk," he said. "Sit down." He went to his desk and lowered his bulk into the big executive chair. "How are you settling in?"

I found a chair and sat on the edge of it. Parnell made me nervous. Even Chick, who had worked with him for years, admitted that he was also nervous in Parnell's presence.

"Fine, sir," I said.

"Chick tells me you are useful. You should be. Your father was a good operator. You've come from a good school."

"Thank you, sir."

"I've a job for you. Read this," and he pushed a letter across his desk towards me.

The letter was written in a sprawling handwriting and the paper was slightly soiled as if written on a dirty desk or table.

Alligator Lane.
West Creek.

Dear Colonel Parnell,

When my son was killed in battle, you were good enough to write to me, telling me how he died, and that you had recommended him to be awarded the Medal of Honor which was granted to him posthumously.

I understand you have a Detective Agency in Paradise City, not far from where I live. I need a detective. My grandson has disappeared. The local police show no interest. I must know what has happened to the boy. I enclose one hundred dollars to hire one of your men to find the boy. I am unable to pay more, but rely on you to do this for me because of what my son did for your regiment.

Yours faithfully,
Frederick Jackson.

Having talked to Glenda Kerry, who looked after the financial end of the agency together with Charles Edwards, the accountant, I knew the agency never took on a client who wasn't prepared to pay at least $5000 as a retainer, and $1000 a day expenses; I looked at Parnell and raised my eyebrows.

"Yup!" Parnell said, reading my thoughts. "We get a few letters like this, asking to hire operators: people with no money, and Glenda gives them a polite brush off, but this is different." He paused to light a cigar. Then he went on, "Ever heard of Mitch Jackson?"

"Yes, sir."

4

I had only a vague recollection, but felt this was the time to look intelligent.

"Mitch Jackson was my staff sergeant: the best soldier I've ever had." Parnell screwed up his eyes while he thought. "Some man! He was too efficient and brave to last. So, we are going to help his old man, Dirk. We'll take his hundred bucks and, by taking it, he is our client. We are going to give him our best service. Understand?"

"Yes, sir."

"This assignment is going to be your pigeon," Parnell went on, giving me his military stare. "Go and see the old coot and find out what's biting him. Treat him as a VIP. Understand?"

"Yes, sir."

"Get the dope, then come back and report to me. We'll see what we can do when we get the details. You get off tomorrow morning." He studied me. "This will be your chance to show me how you are shaping, so let's have a nice, smooth performance. Right?" He tossed a hundred-dollar bill across the desk.

"Use this for expenses." He gave a sly grin. "And not a word about this to Glenda. If she knew I was taking on a hundred-dollar client she would split her pantyhose."

"Yes, sir."

"Okay, Dirk. Let's have some fast action. We don't want to waste a lot of time, but I want this tied up."

With a wave of his hand, he dismissed me.

I returned to the office I shared with Chick. He was going through a fat file which I knew covered all the employees of the self-service store we were watching.

He looked up.

"What's new?"

I sat down and told him.

5

"Mitch Jackson?" He released a long, low whistle. "Some man! I served with him when he was staff under the colonel. I didn't know he was married. Must have been when we had a month's leave. He never told us." He looked thoughtfully at me. "Did the Colonel tell you how Mitch died?"

"He didn't say."

"It's something that was a military secret. You had better know in case, when talking to his father, you drop a bollock. Just keep this to yourself."

"How did he die then?"

"It was a typical Army screw-up. A patrol of twenty men were sent into a big patch of jungle where it was thought the Viets were hiding. We had been losing too many men by sniper fire and we were held up in the advance. The brigade came to this patch of jungle, around a thousand acres: ideal for snipers. The colonel sent in this patrol, led by a veteran sergeant. Their job was to test the ground and flush out the snipers. The rest of the brigade waited on a hill, looking down on this patch of jungle. Word had gone back to headquarters that the brigade was held up. So the situation was these twenty men were going into the jungle and the brigade was waiting and watching. Mitch wanted to go with the patrol. He always wanted to be in the forefront of any action, but the colonel wouldn't let him. The patrol was scarcely into the jungle when a signal came from headquarters that bombers were on their way and they had orders to blast the patch of jungle with napalm. Some goddamn Air Force general hadn't seen the colonel's signal that the patrol was going in, and had ordered out his bombers. It was too late to call off the bombers. They could already be heard approaching. Mitch got into a jeep and drove down with the colonel yelling to him to come back, but Mitch was thinking of those twenty kids and nothing

6

could stop him. He drove into the jungle until the jeep smashed into a tree, then he ran in, bawling to retreat. Seventeen youngsters got out as the bombers began to plaster the patch with napalm. We saw Mitch come out with them, then he stopped, found three were missing. He sent the seventeen running up the hill and he went back into the jungle." Chick blew out his cheeks. "By then the jungle was on fire and lumps of burning napalm spreading. It was the maddest and bravest thing I don't ever want to see again."

"What happened?"

"That's how Mitch died: saving the lives of seventeen kids. What we found of him was shovelled into a burlap bag. Just his steel identity bracelet to tell us we had found him."

"And the other three?"

"Nothing: bits of bone, a lump or two of cooked meat, and, what made it worse, there were no Viets in the jungle. They must have pulled out hours before we arrived. It was a cover-up. What we call in the Agency a fig-leaf job. The Air Force general who had ordered the strike was transferred. The colonel raised hell, but the top brass muzzled him. The citation for the Medal of Honor, which the colonel insisted Mitch should have, said it was for saving the lives of seventeen soldiers, and Mitch had been instantly killed by a Viet sniper while getting the men out of the ambush." Chick shrugged. "It made nicer reading for his father than what really happened."

"Well, thanks for telling me. I'll watch it when I talk to his father."

Chick pulled the file towards him.

"Yeah," he said. "I wonder what the father is like. If he's anything like his son, you watch it."

The following morning, equipped with an overnight case and a large-scale map, I set off in one of the office cars for West Creek.

Although I had spent most of my life in Florida, this would be new country to me. The map told me that West Creek was a few miles to the north of Lake Placid. The guidebook I had consulted told me West Creek had a population of 56 and it survived by breeding frogs which I learned fetched fancy prices during the winter when the frogs were difficult to catch. There seemed to be a constant demand for frogs' legs by the swank restaurants along the coast.

The drive took a little over three hours and I stopped off at Searle, a thriving farming town, growing tomatoes, peppers, Irish potatoes and squash, and which was according to my map a few miles from West Creek. I had had only a cup of coffee for breakfast and I was hungry. Besides, it is always smart to chat up the locals before moving onto the scene to be investigated.

I went into a clean-looking cafe-restaurant and sat down at a table by one of the windows, overlooking the busy main street, crammed with trucks, loaded with vegetables.

A girl came over and gave me a sexy smile: a nice-looking chick, blonde, wearing tight jeans and a tighter T-shirt.

"What's yours?" she asked, placing her hands on the table and leaning forward so her breasts did a jig behind the shirt.

"What's the special?" I asked, restraining the urge to poke one of her breasts with a forefinger.

"Chicken hash, and the chicken didn't die of old age."

"Okay. I'll take it."

I watched her swing her neat little bottom as she made for the kitchen. Even a backwater like Searle could provide excitement.

I became aware that there was a tall, elderly man with a heavy white moustache, stained yellow with tobacco smoke, up at the bar. He was pushing seventy and he wore a soiled Stetson hat and a dark suit that was nickel-plated with age. He looked at me and I gave him a nod and a smile. He stared for a long moment, then, picking up his glass, he came over to me.

"Howdy, stranger," he said and sat down. "Don't often see strange faces in this neck of the woods."

"Just passing through," I told him. "Taking a look. I'm on vacation."

"Is that right?" he sipped his drink. "You could do worse. Plenty of interesting things to see. One time this district was a'gator country. Still a few to be seen off Peace River."

"I saw some at Everglades. Interesting."

The girl brought the chicken hash and slapped the plate down before me. She looked at the elderly man.

"You want something or are you seat-warming?"

"I have something," the elderly man said and lifted his glass. "If I were ten years younger I would have something for you."

"Make it thirty years younger and I might be interested," she said with a sexy grin and swished away.

The elderly man shook his head.

"The young today have no respect for their elders."

I could have said the young today had no reason to respect their elders, but I stopped short. I wasn't going to get into that kind of discussion.

I began on the chicken hash.

"A'gator country," the elderly man said. "You ever heard of Alligator Platt? No, I guess you're too young. He is folklore around here."

I munched, finding the chicken *had* died of old age.

"Folklore?"

"Yeah. Know what? Platt would hide along the bank until an a'gator surfaced, then he would dive in and grapple with the reptile. He would get astride it and hook his thumbs into its eyes. Never failed, but it needed a lot of strength and guts. He said shooting a'gators was a waste of a bullet."

"Those were the days," I said.

"There was only one man who could do what Platt used to do, but, eventually, he got unlucky. Platt died in his bed, but old Fred Jackson lost both his legs."

Time and again, when I was on a job and got into conversation with one of the natives, I struck gold, but not this fast.

Casually, I said, "Fred Jackson? Would he be the father of Mitch Jackson, the war hero?"

The elderly man looked sharply at me.

"That's right. How did you know Fred lives up here?"

"I didn't. You told me." I looked directly at him. "I didn't get your name. I'm Dirk Wallace."

"Silas Wood. Glad to know you, Mr Wallace. What's your line?"

"I'm in the Agency business."

"Agency? What's that mean?"

"I collect information: background material for writers."

He looked impressed.

"Is that right? I'm retired. Use to have a tomato-farm, but there's too much competition these days. I sold out."

"Tell me, Mr Wood, did Fred Jackson lose his legs after or before he lost his son?"

The question seemed to puzzle him. He pulled at his long nose and thought about it.

Finally, he said, "Well, since you ask, Fred lost his legs when Mitch was a nipper. Fred must be seventy-eight now if he's a day. Mitch did most everything for Fred until he got drafted. By then, Fred had got used to being legless. He became real handy getting around on his stumps. He is still the best frog-catcher around here and he makes a tidy living."

"You knew Mitch?"

"Knew him?" Wood again pulled at his nose. "Everyone around here knew Mitch. I nor anyone else thought he would turn out to be hero. It just shows you you can't judge kids: like that girl. She could settle down, but she won't ever be a national hero ... that's for sure."

"Mitch was wild?"

Wood finished his drink and gazed unhappily at the empty glass.

This was a hint, so I took his glass and waved it at the girl, who was resting her breasts on the bar counter and watching us.

She brought a refill and set it before Wood.

"That's your second," she said, "and your last." Looking at me, she went on, "He can't carry more than two, so don't tempt him," and she returned to the bar.

Wood gave me a sly grin.

"Like I said, the young have no respect for their elders."

"I was asking ... was Mitch wild?"

I had finished the chicken hash, not sorry the meal was over. My jaw felt tired.

"Wild? That's not the right word. He was a real hellion." Wood sipped his drink. "He was always in trouble with the sheriff. No girl was safe within miles of him. He was a thief and a poacher. I'd hate to tell you how many tomatoes he stole from my farm or how many chickens disappeared or how many frogs vanished from other farmers' frog barrels.

The sheriff knew he was doing the stealing, but Mitch was too smart for him. Then there was this fighting. Mitch was real vicious. He would often come into town in the evening and pick a quarrel. Nothing he liked better than to fight. Once, four young guys who thought they were tough ganged up on him, but they all landed in hospital. I had no time for him. Frankly, he scared me. He even scared the sheriff. The town was glad when he got drafted and we saw the last of him." Wood paused to sip his drink. "But one can forgive and forget when a guy wins the Medal of Honor. Right now the town is proud of him. Let bygones be bygones I say." He winked. "Many a girl cried herself to sleep when the news broke that he was dead. He seemed to be able, by just snapping his fingers, for the girls to spread their legs."

I was absorbing all this with interest.

"And his father? Was he like his son?"

"Fred? No. He was a worker and he was honest. Mind you, he was tough, but straight. When he lost his legs, he changed. Before that happened, he would come into town and be good company, but not after losing his legs. He no longer welcomed visitors. He still hunted frogs with the help of Mitch, but he stopped coming to town and anyone who went up there got short shrift. Even now, at his age, he still hunts frogs. Once a week, a truck goes up there and takes his catch. I guess he must live on rabbits and fish. I haven't seen him for a good ten years."

"How about Mitch's mother? Is she alive?"

"I wouldn't know. No one around here ever saw her. The story is some woman tourist went up there to take photographs of Fred and the a'gators. That was when he was in his prime. I guess he was like Mitch with women. Anyway, one day, Fred got landed with a baby: left outside

12

his shack. That was Mitch. Mind you, I won't swear to any of this, but that was the story going around Searle. Fred brought him up the hard way, but he made him attend school. When Fred lost his legs, it was Mitch who saved him. From then on, Mitch looked after his father until Fred could stump around on his thighs. That's the only good thing I can say for Mitch: he sure was fond of Fred: no question about that."

"Interesting," I said.

"That's right. It gave the town a lot to talk about. Not every town our size has a national hero. Then there was the grandson."

I showed mild interest.

"You mean Mitch's son?"

"That's right. It was a mystery. Some nine years ago, a kid arrived here. He was around eight years of age. I remember seeing him arrive. He looked like a little bum: as if he had been on the road for days: dirty, long hair, his shoes falling to bits. He had an old battered suitcase, tied up with string. I felt sorry for him. I like kids. I asked him what he was doing here. He spoke well. He said he was looking for Fred Jackson, who was his grandpa. I couldn't have been more surprised. I told him where Fred lived. The kid looked starved so I offered him a meal, but he was very polite and said he wanted to get to his grandpa quickly. Josh, our mailman, was setting off in his truck and I got him to take the kid. At the time, Mitch was in the Army. There was a lot of talk in the town as you can imagine. The schoolteacher went up to see Fred. For a change, Fred saw and talked to him. The upshot was the kid, Johnny Jackson, attended school: riding down here on a cycle."

"Was Johnny like his father?"

"Not a scrap. He was a nice-looking, quiet, polite kid, maybe a bit soft, but he was smart at school. The kids hadn't much time for him. He was a loner and never talked about Mitch. When the kids asked him, he told them he had never seen his father. He had been born after his father had gone overseas. When the news broke that Mitch had been killed and had won the medal, the kid didn't turn up at school. By then, he was fourteen. The schoolteacher went up there and Fred told him to get the hell out and stay out. After that, and that was six years ago, no one has seen the kid. My guess is he got tired of living rough and took off. Can't say I blame him. Old Fred really lived rough." Wood finished his drink, sighed, then took out an old silver watch and consulted it. "I must get moving, Mr Wallace. My wife has a hot meal for me, always dead on one o'clock. She gets kind of peevish if I'm late." He shook my hand. "Have a good vacation. I hope to see you around. We could have another drink together."

When he had gone I signalled to the girl for coffee. By now, there were a number of truckers eating: none of them looked my way and I wasn't interested in them. I was only interested in the natives.

The girl brought the coffee.

"Don't believe everything old Wood tells you," she said, setting down the cup. "He's senile. What was he yakking about?"

"Mitch Jackson."

Her face lit up and she got that soppy expression kids get when they are turned on.

"There was a real man!" She closed her eyes and sighed. "Mitch! He's been dead now for six years, but his memory lingers on. I only saw him once: that was when I was a kid, but I'll never forget him."

"Wood said he was a hellion. In my book, if a guy wins the Medal of Honor he has to be great." I fed her this line because I could see by her besotted face Mitch meant more to her than Elvis Presley meant to millions of teenagers.

"You can say that again! Who would have thought his son would be such a drip?"

I stirred my coffee. It seemed my day to pan gold.

"Was he?"

"We were at school together. All the girls were after him because Mitch was his father. What a drip! He just ran like a frightened rabbit."

A trucker bawled for his lunch. The girl grimaced and left me.

I sipped the coffee and thought over what I had learned. According to Silas Wood, Fred's grandson hadn't been seen since Mitch had died. Again according to Wood the town's opinion was the boy, Johnny Jackson, had left. This didn't make sense to me. If the boy had left six years ago, why should Fred Jackson write to Parnell now to start an investigation to find him after this long lapse?

I decided to inquire around some more before setting off for Alligator Lane. I paid my check and went out onto the busy street. Pausing to look around, I saw a notice with an arrow pointing:

MORGAN & WEATHERSPOON.
Best Frog saddles.

Fred Jackson was in the frog business. I could pick up some information so I followed the direction of the arrow down an alley to double gates on which was another sign:

MORGAN & WEATHERSPOON.
FROGS
YOU HAVE ARRIVED: ENTER.

The stench coming over the high wooden fence turned my stomach. I pushed open one of the gates and walked into a big courtyard where two open trucks were parked. Each truck was loaded with barrels and from the barrels came croaking noises.

Across the way was a concrete building. Through the big window, I could see a man in a white coat, working at a desk. I walked up the three steps, pushed open the door and entered a small, air-conditioned office. I hastily closed the door before the stench in the yard could invade.

The man at the desk gave me a friendly smile. He was around forty-six, thin, with thinning black hair and sharp features.

"What can I do for you?" he asked, getting to his feet. He offered his hand. "Harry Weatherspoon."

"Dirk Wallace," I said, shaking hands. "Mr Weatherspoon, I'm here to waste a little of your time, but I hope you will be indulgent."

His smile widened, but his small, shrewd eyes regarded me speculatively.

"Right now, Mr Wallace, I have time. In half an hour, I'll be busy, but at this moment I am digesting lunch, so take a seat and tell me what's on your mind."

We sat down.

"I work for an agency that collects information for writers and journalists," I said, using the never failing cover story. "I'm the guy who feeds them with facts. They write up the facts and make millions. I don't." I gave him a rueful smile. "So, I'm investigating the background of Mitch

Jackson, our national hero, his father and frogs as an important magazine is planning to do a feature on Mitch."

He scratched his thinning pate.

"I would have thought that was stale news. There's been a lot written about Mitch Jackson."

"Well, you know how it is, Mr Weatherspoon. I'm looking for a new angle."

He shrugged.

"Well, I can tell you about frogs, but I have never met Mitch Jackson. From what I've heard, I'm not sorry. Now, frogs. You notice the smell? Well, you get used to it. Frogs are smelly and live in smelly places. Frog legs or saddles as we call them in the trade, bring high prices. Personally, I don't like them, but, served in a garlic sauce, there are a lot of wealthy people who do like them. It's quite a flourishing industry. Here, we collect from the frog farmers, process and sell to restaurants." He leaned back in his chair and I could see by his animated expression frogs were close to his heart. "The trick, of course, is to catch the frogs. Happily, that's not my headache. Now, Fred Jackson has been, for thirty years, our best supplier, not only in quantity, but now I don't rely on him so much. He's getting old ... aren't we all?" He favoured me with another wide smile. "Frog farmers work this way: they find the right kind of land with swamp and ponds and either rent it or buy. Fred Jackson was smart. He bought his land years ago for next to nothing. Frogs live on insects. Breeders, like Jackson, throw rotten meat around the pond. The meat attracts blowflies. Frogs like blowflies. While they are catching blowflies, the farmers catch them. Jackson is an expert. Not satisfied with a daylight catch, he's installed electric light around his ponds to attract moths and bugs. So the frogs also eat at night and Jackson is there to catch them. A female frog lays anything from ten to thirty thousand eggs a year. Ninety days later, tadpoles arrive. It takes two years before a frog is fit to eat." He smiled again. "Lecture over."

"Thank you," I said. "That's just what I want." I paused, then went on, "You tell me that you never met Mitch Jackson, and yet you said, in spite of him being a national hero, you're not sorry. Would you explain that?"

He looked a little shifty, then shrugged.

"You should understand, Mr Wallace, I am not a native of this town. It has taken me some time to get accepted. I bought a partnership with Morgan who retired and has lately died. I run this business. Mitch Jackson has a big reputation here because he won the medal, so I wouldn't want to be quoted. The kids here adore his memory, so what I'll tell you is strictly off the record."

"No problem," I said. "You don't get mentioned if that's what you want."

"That's what I want." He stared hard at me, then continued, "I came to Searle after Mitch Jackson had died. I heard plenty about him. The natives had been scared of him. According to them he had been a vicious thug, but, when he won the medal, the town made him folklore and the girls here shot their stupid lids and now treat his memory as if he was some god-awful pop singer."

I let that one drift. When I was a kid, my idol was Sinatra. Kids have to have idols.

"If you want the inside dope about Mitch Jackson, you should ask Abe Levi," Weatherspoon went on. "He's one of my truckers who collects frog barrels up north. He's been collecting from Fred Jackson for years." He looked at his watch. "He'll be in the processing shed right now. Do you want to talk to him?"

"Sure, and thanks, Mr Weatherspoon. Just one other thing: anything you can tell me about Fred Jackson?" He shook his head.

"No. I've never seen him. I heard he lost both legs, fighting an alligator. While he was recovering, Mitch did the frog catching, then Fred got mobile again. His catch has been falling off recently, but that's to be expected at his age. From what I hear, he's tough and honest."

I got to my feet.

"I'll talk to Levi."

He pointed through the window.

"That big shed there. He'll be taking his lunch." He stood up. "Nice meeting you, Mr Wallace. If there's anything else you want to know about frogs, you know where to find me."

We shook hands and I walked out into the stench.

In the shed, where a number of coloured girls were dissecting frogs, a sight and smell that made me want to gag, I found a man, around sixty-five, eating out of a can of beans. That anyone could eat in that awful stink beat me, but this man, short, squat, powerfully built with a greying beard and none too clean, seemed to be enjoying his meal.

I gave him the same story as I had given Weatherspoon about collecting information for an agency. He listened while he ate, then regarded me with grey eyes that lit up with the cunning light of the poor.

For years I had been digging for information and I knew that look.

"Mr Weatherspoon tells me," I said, "you could give me information. I don't expect information for nothing. Would five bucks interest you?"

"Ten bucks would be better," he said promptly.

I took a five-dollar bill from my wallet and waved it in his direction.

"Five to start. Let's see how we go."

He snapped the bill from my fingers the way a lizard snaps up a fly.

"Okay, mister. What do you want to know?"

"Tell me about Fred Jackson. You've known him for years, I'm told."

"That's right, and the more I see him the less I want to. He's a mean old cuss. Okay, I guess most people would turn mean if they lost their legs, but Fred has always been mean."

"Mean? Are you saying he is close with money?"

"I didn't say that, although he is close, but he has a mean nature. The kind of man who would do dirt to his best friend and think nothing of it." Levi squinted at me. "Not that Fred ever had any friends. He has a mean character, like his son."

"His son won the Medal of Honor."

Levi snorted.

"He won it because he's tough, mean and vicious. He never cared a damn what he walked into. I don't call that brave. I call it stupid. The Jacksons are rotten. I've no time for either of them. I've been up to Jacksons' cabin every week for more than twenty years. Never once did either of them offer me a beer. Never once did either of them give me a hand loading the barrels, and frog barrels are mighty heavy. Mind you, now Fred's lost his legs, I don't expect help, but Mitch, when he was around, watched me strain my guts out and just grinned." He snorted. "Other frog-farmers always give me a beer and a hand, but never the Jacksons." He looked inside the tin of beans, scraped, found a couple of beans and ate them. "All this talk about

20

Mitch Jackson being a national hero makes me want to puke. The fact is the town's well rid of him."

I wasn't getting anything more from him than I had already got from Weatherspoon.

"Did you meet the grandson?"

"Just once. I saw him up there. I arrived in the truck and he was washing clothes in a tub. I guess Fred made him earn his keep. As soon as he saw me, he went into the shack and Fred came out. I never spoke to the kid. I guess he got choked living with Fred and took off when Mitch was killed. I only saw him this once. That's close on six years ago."

"He would be around fourteen years of age?"

"I guess. A skinny kid, nothing like either of the Jacksons. I've often wondered if he was really Mitch's son. Mitch had the kind of face you see in police mug shots. This kid had class. The kids at his school said that. They said he was different. I guess he sure must have took after his mother."

"Know anything about her?"

Levi shook his head.

"No one does. Probably some piece Mitch screwed. Could have been any girl around the district. He never left the girls alone. I dunno, maybe the kid had the same itch. I remember seeing a girl up there." He thought, then shook his head. "That was only four months ago, long after the kid was thought to have taken off."

Not showing my interest, I said casually, "Tell me about the girl."

"I only caught a glimpse of her. She was washing clothes the way the kid washed clothes in a tub outside the cabin. As soon as I drove around the bend, she ran into the cabin and kept out of sight. When Fred turned up, I asked him if he had hired help, but he just growled at me: no more than I could expect from him. I thought he must have hired a girl from the town to replace the kid. I admit I was nosey and I asked around, but no one knew of any girl working for Fred." He shrugged. "I never saw her again."

"What was she like? How old?"

He licked the spoon he was holding, then put it in his pocket.

"Young, thin with long yellow hair. I noticed her hair. It reached to her waist and was dirty."

"What was she wearing?"

"Jeans and something. I don't remember. Maybe Johnny was there after all and she was shacking up with him. Fred wouldn't have cared. He didn't care about the way Mitch went on with girls." He paused, then with a sly grin, asked, "How am I doing?"

"One more question. I'm told Mitch was a loner. Didn't he even have one friend?"

Levi scratched his dirty beard.

"Yeah, there was a jerk Mitch went around with. Like Mitch: no good." He gazed into space. "Right now, I don't seem to remember his name."

I produced another five-dollar bill, but kept it out of his reach. He eyed the bill, scratched his beard some more, then nodded.

"Yeah. I remember now ... Syd Watkins. He got drafted the same time as Mitch. The town was glad to see both of them go. His ma and dad were respectable. They ran the grocery store at Searle, but when she died he retired. He couldn't run the store without her and Syd never did a day's work in his life."

"Mitch and Syd were pals?"

Levi grimaced.

"I wouldn't know about that. They were thieving partners and went around together. When Mitch picked a quarrel, Syd never joined in. He just watched. You could say he was the brains and Mitch was the brawn."

"After the war, did he come home?"

"No. From time to time, I have a drink with his dad. The old man is always expecting to hear from his son, but, so far, never has. All he knows is Syd was discharged from the Army, came back to the States and then dropped out of sight. It's my bet he's up to no good."

I brooded for a long moment, then gave him the other five-dollar bill.

"If I think of anything, I'll see you again," I said. I was longing to get out of that shed and breathe some clean smelling air. "Are you always here at this time?"

"Sure am," he said and put the bill in his pocket.

"How do I get to Fred's place?"

"You got a car?"

I nodded.

"It's some five miles from here." He gave me detailed directions. "You be careful with Fred ... he's mean."

With a lot to think about, I walked to where I had parked my car and set off for Alligator Lane.

As I drove up the main street, I passed the sheriff's office. I wondered if I should stop off and introduce myself. From past experience, I had learned local sheriffs could be hostile to an operator, nosing around their territory, but I decided I should first talk to Fred Jackson. He had hired the agency to find his grandson. Maybe he wanted to keep the investigation confidential.

Abe Levi had warned me that Alligator Lane wasn't signposted. He had told me to look out for a narrow turning off the highway, half concealed by sparkleberry bushes. By taking it slow with no traffic to bother me, I came upon the turning and swung the car onto a dirt lane, twisting and turning like a dying snake and bordered either side with dense forest. After a couple of miles, the lane widened: a place where trucks could wait before driving down the one-way lane to the highway.

I knew I was approaching Jackson's cabin by the distant sound of the croaking of frogs. I kept on, then the lane narrowed again and turned sharply to the right. I edged the car forward and before me was a wooden cabin, a water well and a bucket near the entrance door, a bench under one of the grimy windows and a frog barrel.

I had arrived.

I stopped the car, cut the engine, then tapped the horn. Nothing happened. The only sound was the croaking of frogs.

I waited, then tapped the horn again.

Still nothing happened.

I told myself that Fred Jackson was out hunting frogs. I got out of the car. The air was steamy hot. The trees cut off any breeze that might have been around. The continuous frog noise grated on my nerves. There was something almost human in that noise: like very old men clearing phlegm from their throats.

I lit a cigarette as I studied the cabin. It had been well constructed in pine wood. From the look of the outside, it would have a big living-room and probably two bedrooms.

I saw the front door stood ajar.

The heat was beginning to make me sweat: that and the frog orchestra and the loneliness of the place increased my tension. There was an eerie atmosphere that hung over the place that I could feel.

I wandered to the front door and rapped. Nothing happened, so, after rapping again and waiting, I pushed the door open. The shrill squeak of rusty hinges gave me a start.

I peered into the gloom of a large room, furnished with heavy junk you see in market auctions and which no one, these days, wanted.

I saw Fred Jackson sitting at the big table. It had to be Jackson because the old bearded man at the table had no legs. Before him was a plate of some kind of stew. I couldn't see much of it as it was covered with a canopy of excited blowflies.

My eyes shifted to an enormous brown and green bullfrog that sat at the far end of the table, watching the blowflies. It looked at me with glittering black eyes, then leapt into the air, coming in my direction, making me duck. It landed on the floor with a plop and was gone.

"Mr Jackson ..." I began, then stopped.

The man at the table continued to sit motionless.

By now, my eyes were growing accustomed to the gloom. I moved into the room.

"Mr Jackson ..."

The blowflies buzzed, lifted, then resettled on what was on the plate.

Then I saw blood trickling down Jackson's face, slowly and congealing.

I saw the bullet hole in the middle of Jackson's dirty forehead.

He was now as dead as his son, but much more neatly killed.

2

I paused in the open doorway of the sheriff's office and looked around. The scene was familiar. You'll see it again and again on TV movies: the gun rack; handcuffs hanging from hooks; the two desks and three unoccupied cells.

An atmosphere of inactivity and boredom hung over the office like a mantle of dust.

At the big desk facing me, Sheriff Tim Mason, according to the plaque on the desk, sat like an enthroned Buddha. It seemed to me only his soiled khaki blouse, on which was the sheriff's star, and his trousers held his fat together. He was possibly the fattest man I have seen and, what was more, his flushed and veined face, bloodshot eyes and the sweat dripping from under his Stetson told me he was a bottle-hitter.

At the other desk was what seemed to me a blue eyed boy who could have been Mickey Rooney's double when Rooney was playing juvenile roles. The plaque on his desk told me he was Deputy Sheriff Bill Anderson.

Sheriff Mason stared at me as if he were trying to get me in focus. Deputy Sheriff Anderson got to his feet. He was pint-size, but he had plenty of beef and muscle around his shoulders.

"Something I can do for you?" he asked with a hesitant smile. I guessed he would be around twenty-three or -four years of age.

I moved into the office and to his desk.

"Reporting the murder of Frederick Jackson of Alligator Lane," I said.

Deputy Sheriff Anderson reared back as if I had pasted one on his chin.

"Who the hell are you?" Mason demanded in a loud, bullying voice.

I took out my wallet, selected one of my business cards and, moving over to him, put the card on his desk.

He picked up the card with a shaky hand, peered at it for a long moment, then managed to get the print in focus.

"A goddamn peeper!" His fat face turned vicious. "I don't like peepers! What are you doing in my town?"

"I am reporting the murder of Frederick Jackson, the frog-farmer," I said loudly and distinctly.

He read the print on my card again. What I had said apparently hadn't penetrated.

"I don't like peepers," he repeated. "I won't have them in my town. Get out and stay out!"

"I am reporting the murder of Frederick Jackson," I said, raising my voice a tone.

Like an elephant rising off its knees, he got to his feet and came lumbering around the desk.

"You handle this jerk, Bill," he said. "Get rid of him. I've got business up the road," and, moving by me, he waddled out into the hot sunshine and out of sight.

I picked up my card and put it on Anderson's desk. "Is this your usual routine?" I asked. Anderson shuffled his feet, read my card, stared at me, then shook his head.

"You've come at the wrong time, Mr Wallace. The sheriff has to have his medicine at this time and, until he has had it, he doesn't absorb facts."

"Doesn't he keep a bottle here?"

27

"He likes to drink in company. What did you say you were reporting?"

I restrained my impatience with an effort. I told myself I was dealing with hick people in a hick town.

"Frederick Jackson has been murdered."

He flinched.

"I thought you said that, but I can't believe it. Are you sure?"

"He's dead. He's been shot in the head. There's no gun, so someone shot him," I said patiently.

"You've seen him?"

"Just come from his place. You'd better get him to the mortuary. His cabin's like an oven and the blowflies are having a ball."

He turned pale under his tan and sat down abruptly.

"Murdered! This is the first murder we have ever had up here," he muttered.

"Well, you have one now. It'll make a change."

"Jesus! Murder!"

I began to feel sorry for him. He was too young to be a deputy sheriff. He probably had little experience of police work. He could deal with thieving, parking problems, drunkenness and maybe an occasional rape, but murder would be way out of his league.

"I suggest your first move is to call the State police," I said in my soothing voice. "They'll handle it."

His eyes popped wide open.

"I can't do that. Sheriff Mason won't have anything to do with them! He's been sheriff here for twenty years and has never called the State police."

"Now's the time," I said. "You'll have to call them sooner or later, so call them now."

He rubbed his chin with the back of his hand. I could almost hear his brain creak as he thought and I felt more sorry for him. He was being loyal to the old rum-dum. He knew, as I did, that if the State police came up here and took one look at Sheriff Mason it would be curtains for him.

"He's retiring at the end of the year," Anderson said, half to himself. "He's been a fine man, but the bottle caught up with him. He's liked by everyone. They all look the other way when he gets stoned. If the State police ..." He again rubbed his chin and looked helplessly at me.

"I'm reporting a murder," I said. "That lets me out. What you do is your business."

He looked again at my business card.

"You work for Colonel Parnell?"

"That's what the card says."

"It's a marvellous agency. The best."

I was getting bored with him.

"Yeah. It's the best."

"I heard there was a vacancy for an operator. I wrote in." Anderson again rubbed his chin. "But it was filled. I'd give a lot to work for Colonel Parnell. Do you think there'll be another vacancy?"

"Maybe. It depends on the applicant. The colonel is always on the look-out for a smart operator."

"The pay is pretty good, isn't it?"

"Sure."

"It would be a big thing in my life to get a job with Colonel Parnell." He did the chin rubbing act again, not looking at me. He was dreaming ambitious dreams. "I've had it up to here in this small-time town."

"It's going to be big time," I said. "Murder always hits the headlines."

He started as if in his dreams he had forgotten he had a murder in his lap.

"Yes. I hadn't thought of that. Jesus! What do I do?"

"Call the State police before Jackson gets full of maggots."

He went a shade paler.

"I can't do that!" He looked beseechingly at me. "What would you do in my place?"

"Well, if I couldn't call the State police, I'd get an ambulance and a doctor and go up there and take a look," I said. "After all, you are only taking my word for it, aren't you?"

He visibly brightened.

"I'll do that," and he reached for the telephone.

I wandered to the door and looked out onto the busy street while he talked on the telephone. The set-up seemed to me to be right out of the comics, but it did occur to me, by jollying Anderson along, I could get information of value for my report to the colonel.

When he had finished talking, he joined me at the door.

"The ambulance is coming and Dr Steed will be with it. He's our coroner." He looked unsteadily at me. "He's pretty old, but he is the most important citizen here, after the sheriff." He fidgeted, then went on, "I guess you have had a lot of experience with murder cases."

I could see he was longing for me to say yes, so I didn't disappoint him.

"We get all kinds of cases: murder, blackmail, kidnapping. I've had my share."

He looked happy.

"I was wondering. Would you come along with me? You could spot clues I might miss."

"I can't do that. Sheriff Mason wouldn't approve. He doesn't dig peepers. I don't want trouble with him."

"Oh, he won't make trouble for you. Once he has had his shot, he's a different man. I'm not kidding. You caught him at the wrong time. He'll be pleased to have your help."

"You'd better ask him. How long does he take to get tanked?"

"He won't be around for a couple of hours, but there's no need for me to ask him. You won't know him when next you see him. He's the most popular man in our town when he has had some Scotch."

Just then an ancient looking ambulance pulled up. There were two coloured men in white coats and a small man with a white beard and long white hair who had to be pushing seventy-eight. He got out of the ambulance and stood looking at us. His face was like a dried-up apple and he moved with a limp.

"This is Dr Steed," Anderson said and went down to greet the old man.

I waited until Anderson had done his talking, then Steed looked at me with bright, probing eyes.

I joined him and shook his offered hand.

"Old Fred Jackson," he said in a thin, hoarse voice. "That's bad. Murdered, huh? That's worse! Bill has told me about you, young man. We'll be glad of your help. By rights, we should call the State police, but we like to run our little town without outside interference. We will call on your experience."

"I'm ready to co-operate, sir, but the State police will have to be informed. This is murder."

He gave me a sly little smile.

"That's for me to say, young man. Old Fred hadn't much to live for. He could have decided to end his life."

"There's no gun."

31

"Well, we'll see." Steed limped to the ambulance and got in. By now the citizens of Searle were standing and gaping. It was something novel for them to see an ambulance outside the sheriff's office, plus the coroner, plus a stranger.

"We'll go in my car," Anderson said.

I joined him in the old Chevvy and he followed the ambulance up the main street and onto the highway.

"Has Jackson any relations?" I asked.

"He has a grandson, but no one knows where he is. He hasn't anyone else I know of."

"Did Jackson report to you that his grandson had gone missing?"

"Yes, he did, around two months ago. He sent word by the mailman that he wanted to talk to Sheriff Mason. Well, the sheriff went up there. When he came back, he said Fred was making a fuss about nothing. The kid must have got choked living with Fred and had taken off. Mason said it wasn't worth bothering the State police. They have enough missing people to deal with."

"You said Fred got word to the sheriff by the mailman. Did Fred get mail?"

"I believe so. I wouldn't know." He looked at me. "Think that's important? I mean do you think him getting mail is a clue?"

"Could be. It just struck me as odd that an old recluse like Fred should get mail."

"I could ask Josh: he's our mailman."

"Do that. There's no rush."

By this time, we were driving up the narrow lane leading to Fred Jackson's cabin. The ambulance had stirred up a lot of dust and Anderson had to drive at a crawl.

When he finally pulled up outside the cabin, the two coloured men were getting a stretcher out of the ambulance. I walked to the entrance of the cabin.

Dr Steed was standing over what was left of Frederick Jackson. Blowflies swarmed around his hat. The smell in the room made my stomach cringe.

"See, young man," he said and pointed to the floor by the legs of the chair in which Fred was sitting. "Something you missed."

Lying on the floor, half under the chair, was a small handgun: a .22 Beretta.

"Just as I thought," Dr Steed went on, a smug expression on his old, wrinkled face. "The poor fellow took his life. Murder?" He gave a croaking little chuckle. "Young man, you should be more careful. It's suicide as plain as the nose on my face."

As an unauthorized observer being told I had started a murder scare by the most important citizen in Searle, I kept my mouth shut, but I did know the gun hadn't been there when I had left the cabin to report to the sheriff. That I knew for sure.

As Anderson and I followed the ambulance, containing the remains of Frederick Jackson down the narrow lane, Anderson said, reproach in his voice, "Excuse me, Mr Wallace, but I'm surprised you didn't see the gun. I really thought we had a murder case to solve."

"Cheer up," I said, taking out my pack of cigarettes. "You still could have." I lit up and stared through the dust.

"Dr Steed says it is a clear case of suicide."

"That's what *he* said."

Anderson began his chin rubbing routine.

"Don't you think it is?"

33

"Anything can happen in this crazy world. Old Fred was eating his lunch. Then he stopped eating and decided to shoot himself. He promptly shot himself and then hid the gun. After I had found him dead, he took the gun from its hiding place and put it under his chair, then he went back to being dead again. As I say, anything can happen in this crazy world."

He drove in silence for some minutes, then he said, "You must be kidding, Mr Wallace."

"The gun wasn't there when I found Jackson. This smells of a fig-leaf job."

"Fig-leaf? I'm not with you."

"Look, Bill, are you really serious that you want to work for Colonel Parnell?"

"Serious?" His voice shot up: "I told you: I'd give anything in the world to get out of Searle and to be one of Colonel Parnell's operators."

"Okay. You co-operate with me and I'll co-operate with you," I said, flicking cigarette ash out of the car's window. "A strong recommendation from me would have a lot of pull. The Colonel is always on the lookout for a co-operative, smart man with police training."

"You can rely on me, Mr Wallace," Anderson said earnestly. "You just tell me what you want. Honestly, Mr Wallace, you can rely on me."

"Fine. I just said this is a fig-leaf job. We Parnell operators use a special jargon of our own. When we say it's a fig-leaf job, we mean it is a cover-up job. Since Adam bit the apple, he used a fig-leaf to cover his equipment. Get it? Fig-leaf: cover-up."

"You think Jackson's death is a cover-up job?"

"I know it is. This is murder, Bill. Make no mistake about that. Here's what could have happened: the killer could have been still around when I arrived at the cabin. When I left, he could have returned to the cabin and planted the gun. I'm not sold on this idea, but it's possible. I like the idea better that Dr Steed planted the gun. He knew if Jackson had been murdered, the State police would have to be called and that would be the end of Sheriff Mason. So, I like the idea that, when you told him on the phone that Jackson had been murdered, he collected the gun, got ahead of us and planted the gun to give Mason a fig-leaf."

"Dr Steed would never do such a thing!" Anderson gasped.

"Look, Bill, you're young. These things happen. Old friends are loyal to each other. Why should Steed worry about an old man like Jackson getting murdered: a murder that would get his pal Mason into trouble? A suicide keeps the State police out of it. Anyway, murder is police business, not mine. My business is to find Jackson's grandson. Jackson hired the Agency to do just that. But, remember, Bill, if you really want to work with our Agency, I expect you to co-operate."

"Jesus! This is a bit much for me, Mr Wallace, but you sure can rely on my co-operation."

"Then all you have to do is to keep your mouth shut and your ears and eyes open," I said, looking at his young, worried face. "I've alerted you, but say nothing, leave all this to Dr Steed."

Half an hour later, we were sitting around Sheriff Mason's desk: Dr Steed, Anderson and myself.

I thought as I looked at Mason's fat, benign face that it was remarkable what a pint of Scotch could do for a man. Mason, oozing sweat, now looked like a happy Santa Claus.

He had listened to Dr Steed's report, humming under his breath, then he beamed at me.

"So we have a little trouble," he said. "Mr Wallace, let me tell you I have heard of Colonel Parnell. I'm proud to meet one of his operators." He leaned forward and patted my arm. "A great agency. Great operators."

"Thank you," I said.

"A little mistake, huh?" He screwed up his pig-like eyes and released a soft belch. "No matter how smart you are, you can always make a little mistake. Right?"

"Sure," I said, my expression wooden.

He then looked at Dr Steed.

"Now, Larry, you went up there and you tell me that poor old fella shot himself ... right?"

"No doubt about it," Dr Steed said, shaking his head mournfully. "I'm not surprised, Tim. The poor old fella lived in bad conditions, he had lost his grandson and he was lonely. You know, thinking about it, it's a merciful end. I don't stand in judgement of him. To be without legs, no one to take care of him ... a merciful end."

"Yeah." Mason took off his Stetson hat, wiped his forehead, replaced the hat and also looked mournful. "So, there's no need to bring the State police into this sad affair?"

"Certainly not. A suicide doesn't necessitate consulting the State police," Dr Steed said, his voice firm.

Mason beamed and rubbed his hands.

"That's good. I don't like those fellas. When's the inquest, Larry?"

"In a couple of days. I can clear this up quick. We'll have to bury him on the town, Tim. I don't think he had burial money. Still, we can afford it. I guess the town will want to put him away real good."

"You're right: the father of a national hero. You talk to them, Larry." Mason took out his wallet and produced a crumpled five-dollar bill. "I'd like to contribute. I'll leave it to you to raise the rest of the money. We must give him a good send off."

Dr Steed got to his feet as he put the bill in his pocket.

"I've always said, Tim, you have a generous heart. I'll be getting along. You leave the funeral arrangements to me." He turned to me. "Pleasure meeting you, Mr Wallace. I'm sorry your visit to our little town has been so sad. Frederick Jackson was a fine man. His son was a fine man. We, in this little town, are proud of them both."

I stood and shook his hand, then watched him limp to the door. He paused, gave me a sly smile, then limped out into the hot sunshine.

"Well, now, Mr Wallace," Mason said, beaming at me. "I expect you want to move along too. How about a little drink before we say goodbye?" He hoisted a bottle of Scotch out of his desk drawer.

"Not right now," I said, giving him the eye-ball-to-eye-ball treatment. "I'll be around for a day or so. You see, Sheriff, Jackson hired my agency to find his grandson. He paid us, so, although he is dead, he still remains our client."

Mason's eyes went glassy. He lost much of his sweaty happiness.

"No good wasting your time trying to locate the grandson. He could be anywhere. He left this district a good six years ago."

"We still have to try to find him, Sheriff," I said, continuing to stare at him. "Will you object if I ask around or do you want to have a word with Colonel Parnell? I understand you didn't inform the State police the boy has gone missing. Colonel Parnell might want to talk to them."

Mason winced as if he had bitten onto an aching tooth. He hoisted a glass from his desk and poured himself a big shot.

"I don't object, Mr Wallace. You just go ahead, but you are sure wasting your time."

"I'm paid to waste my time," I said, then, without looking at Anderson, who was sitting as quiet as a well-behaved kitten, I walked out into the main street.

I decided, before making any further move, I must report to the colonel. Aware the citizens of Searle were gaping curiously at me, I walked to where I had parked my car and drove fast to Paradise City.

One of the many things my father had taught me was to make a concise, verbal report: omitting no important fact, but cutting out the padding.

Colonel Parnell sat motionless in his executive chair, his eyes half closed, his big hands resting on the snowy blotter on his desk. He listened without interruption until I had told my story of my investigation up at Searle.

The clock on the colonel's desk showed 18.00. Usually, the colonel left the office sharp at 17.30. He was a golf addict and I was pleased my report had interested him enough for him to forget his evening round.

"That's the situation, sir, to date," I concluded, only now realizing I had been talking non-stop for the past half hour.

He looked directly at me.

"You made a good report, Dirk," he said. "Well now, Frederick Jackson still remains our client. We have been hired to find his grandson, but the fact that Jackson has been murdered could complicate the situation."

"The verdict will be suicide, sir," I said. "So no one can accuse us of being involved in a murder case."

He nodded, then picked up a pen and studied it thoughtfully, then again he looked at me.

"I'm wondering if I should pull you off this job and put Chick onto it. He has a lot more experience than you have. This might develop into a real mess."

I tried not to show my disappointment.

"That's up to you, sir."

He gave me a sudden grin.

"So far, you've handled this well, so I'm going to let you stay on the job, but if you run into trouble Chick will take over."

"Thank you, sir."

"Now let us see how the rest of this organization can help. Any ideas?"

"For one thing, I would like to be able to tell Bill Anderson that you are interested and could offer him a job. He is mad keen and this is important to me. I'll have to be careful how I nose around Searle: it is a hotbed of gossip, but Anderson, if sufficiently encouraged, could do some of my leg work without stirring up the mud."

"Yes. You can tell him, as soon as a vacancy comes along, I will certainly give him an interview. If he has really been helpful, tell him he can count on a job with us."

"I'll tell him. Then I want to know what happened to Syd Watkins. I'm told he was discharged from the Army, but after that he dropped out of sight. He hasn't been back to Searle. I think it's important we get a trace on him."

"We'll check him out through the Army's records and the FBI if necessary and see what we come up with."

"I want to know if Mitch Jackson married, when and to whom."

"We should be able to dig into that."

"You told me, sir, that Jackson was the best soldier you had under your command. According to the gossip in Searle, he was no good, vicious, dangerous and a thug."

Parnell frowned. His face hardened and he looked the Army veteran colonel that he was.

"That's nonsense! Mitch was my best staff. I never had complaints about his behaviour. I was told he was popular with his men. He had guts and great courage. No one wins the Medal of Honor without earning it!"

"Okay, sir. Maybe the citizens of Searle are prejudiced. Men can change."

"Yes. War changes men," Parnell said. "In my opinion, Mitch was a fine soldier."

I decided it would be wiser to keep my opinion of Mitch Jackson to myself. Maybe the citizens of Searle knew what they were saying and the colonel was the one who was prejudiced. A Staff sergeant who knew his way around could snow his commanding officer, but that was a fact I wasn't going to mention.

"That's all I can think of for the moment, sir," I said. "I'll return to Searle and put up at the local hotel. My job is to find the grandson, but if I get a lead to Jackson's murder I'll report to you."

"That's it, Dirk. Remember, we don't touch murder cases." He stared thoughtfully at me. "Until you get definite proof that Jackson was murdered, you keep digging."

"Yes, sir."

"You will be on an expense account. I'll talk to Glenda. I want the grandson found."

"Yes, sir."

He nodded, then got to his feet.

"I've missed a round of golf. You play golf, Dirk?"

"I used to, but it got too expensive."

"What did you play to?"

"Well, on my best day, I've shot sixty-eight."

"You did?" He grinned. "We'll have a game together. That's some shooting."

I returned to my office to find Chick Barley clearing his desk.

"How's it going?" he asked. "Let's go and wet our tonsils."

At a near-by bar, I gave him the story I had given the colonel. He listened while he punished a bottle of Scotch.

"Nice going, Dirk. So you have a real job in your lap."

"It could be in your lap, Chick, if I don't get results."

Chick grinned.

"You will. I'd hate to hell to get marooned in a dump like Searle."

"I'm bothered about Mitch Jackson. The colonel's nuts about him, but, from what I hear, Jackson was a real baddie. I'd like to check that out."

Chick regarded me with mild surprise.

"Let me tell you, Dirk, Mitch was the greatest. A guy who did what he did ..."

"Look, let's skip the hero worship," I broke in. "Jackson may have been the white-headed hero to you officers, but I want to check him out by talking to the men who served under him. The rank-and-file. If they say he was the greatest, then he was the greatest. I've served in the Army. I know a Staff sergeant can suck up to officers and be a brute to his men. It's odd to me that the general opinion of the citizens of Searle is they were glad to see the last of him. Okay, I admit war conditions change a man, but, from what I'm hearing, Jackson was a vicious thug. I want to check him out."

Chick poured himself another drink, then he nodded.

"I'll bet my last buck that Mitch was a real man, but you have a point. He was fine with us. Every order we gave him he carried out to perfection. We really could rely on him."

"Did you officers ever talk to the men to find out if they were as happy with Jackson as you were?"

"There was no need to. Damn it, we were a happy regiment. Mitch handled the men, we gave the orders, the whole thing worked."

"I want to check him out. I would like to talk to one of the men who served under him. Know anyone within reaching distance?"

Chick thought, then nodded. "Hank Smith, a coloured man. He has a job on the garbage truck, Miami. I ran into him last year. I didn't remember him, but he remembered me. He insisted I go to his house in West Miami for a drink for old times. When he was in the regiment, he was a good soldier. Come to think of it, he wasn't outgoing when I talked of Mitch and his medal. He just nodded, saying it was a fine thing for the regiment, then he changed the subject." Chick scratched his head. "Well, I don't know. You could have a point. I don't think the colonel would approve, but you could talk to Smith. You'll find him on West Avenue. He has a house at the corner, right."

An hour later, I edged my car into the coloured ghetto of West Miami. The time was 21.10. I had had a hamburger with Chick, then he had gone off on a date, and after returning to my two-room apartment, packing a suitcase for my stay at Searle, I had decided to see if I could talk to Hank Smith.

It was a hot, steamy evening. West Avenue was lined, either side, with small, dilapidated houses. Coloured people sat on their verandas, kids played in the street. I came under the searching stare of many eyes as I pulled up outside a shabby house on the corner, right.

A large, fat woman, her head enveloped in a bright red handkerchief, her floral dress fading from many washes, sat in a rocker, staring into space. Her small black eyes watched me as I got out of the car, pushed open the garden gate and walked up to the veranda. I was aware that some hundreds of eyes from the other verandas were also watching me.

"Mrs Smith?" I asked, coming to rest before the woman. At close quarters, I could see she was around fifty years of age. Her broad, black face had that determined, strong face of a woman who is struggling to keep up a standard and refusing to accept the bitter fact that, for her, standards were slipping out of reach.

She gave me a curt, suspicious nod.

"That's me."

"Is Mr Smith around?"

"What do you want with my husband? If you're selling something, mister, don't bother. I look after our money and I ain't got anything to spare."

A tall, massively built coloured man appeared in the doorway. He had on a clean white shirt and jeans. His close-cropped crinkly hair was shot with grey. His bloodshot black eyes were steady and, as he peeled his thick lips off strong white teeth in a wide smile, he looked amiable.

"You want something, mister?" he asked in a low rumbling voice.

"Mr Smith?"

"Sure ... that's me."

"Mr Smith, I hope I'm not disturbing you. Chick Barley said you might be glad to meet me."

His smile widened.

"Mr Barley is a great man. Sure, I'm always pleased to meet any friend of Mr Barley." He came forward and offered his hand which I shook.

"Dirk Wallace," I said. "I work for Colonel Parnell."

He smiled again.

43

"Another great man. Well, come on in, Mr Wallace. Our neighbours are kind of nosey. Let's have a drink."

"Hank!" his wife said sharply. "Watch with the drink!"

"Relax, Hannah," he said, smiling affectionately at the woman. "A little drink does no harm to good friends."

He led me into a small living-room. The furniture was austere but reasonably comfortable. There were two armchairs, a deal table and three upright chairs.

"Sit you down, Mr Wallace," Smith said, waving to one of the armchairs. "How about a little Scotch?"

"That would be fine," I said.

While he was away, I looked around. There were photographs of him in uniform, his wedding photograph and photographs of two bright-looking kids. He returned with two glasses, clinking with ice and heavy with Scotch.

"And how is Mr Barley?" he asked, giving me one of the glasses. "I haven't seen him for some time."

"He's fine," I said, "and he sends you his best."

Smith beamed and sat down.

"You know, Mr Wallace, we soldiers never had any time for MPs, but Mr Barley was different. Many a time, he'd look the other way when we were in the front line. The guys really liked him."

He raised his glass and saluted me. We drank. The Scotch nearly ripped the skin off my tonsils.

He eyed me.

"A bit strong, huh?" he asked, seeing my eyes water. "We old soldiers like our liquor with a big kick."

I put the glass on the table.

"That's a fact." I managed to grin. "I never did get to 'Nam. It was over before my lot finished training."

"Then I guess you were lucky. 'Nam was no picnic."

I took out my pack of cigarettes and offered it. We both lit up.

"Mr Smith ..."

His smile widened.

"You call me Hank, Mr Wallace. I guess you were an officer ... right?"

"That's old history. Call me Dirk."

"Fine with me." He drank, sighed, then said, "You working for the colonel?"

"Yes. Hank, I've come to see you because Chick said you could help."

"Is that right?" He showed surprise. "Well, sure. Help? What's that mean?"

"Mitch Jackson. Remember him?"

Hank lost his smile.

"I remember him," he said, his voice suddenly cold and flat.

"I'm digging into his past, Hank. It's important. Whatever you say is in confidence. I just want to have your truthful opinion of him."

"Why should you want that?"

"His father died yesterday. There's an investigation. We think Mitch Jackson could be remotely hooked to his father's death."

"You want my truthful opinion?"

"Yes. I assure you if you have anything to tell me it goes no further than these four walls. You have my word."

He moved his big feet while he thought.

"I don't believe in speaking ill of the dead," he said finally. "Especially a Medal of Honor hero."

I sampled the Scotch again. It was still dreadful, but I found I was getting used to its kick.

"How did the men react to Mitch? How did you react?"

He hesitated, then shrugged.

"He had a lot of favourites. That was the trouble. Maybe you don't know, but, when a Staff sergeant has favourites and runs the rest of the men into the ground, he ain't popular. That's what Jackson did. To some he was like a father. To others he was a real sonofabitch."

"How was he with you?"

"I had a real bad time with him: any dirty job, I got it, but it wasn't only me. More than half the batallion got the shitty end of the stick and the other half had it good."

"There must have been a reason."

"There was a reason all right. All those kids who went into that jungle before the bombers arrived were his favourites. That, and no other reason, made him drive after them. Not because he loved them, but because they were worth more than a thousand bucks a week to him, and he was so goddamn greedy he couldn't stand to see his pay-roll being killed. If those kids had been his non-favourites, he wouldn't have moved an inch. That's how he won his medal: trying to save his weekly pay-roll."

"I don't get it, Hank. Why should those kids pay him a thousand bucks a week?"

Hank finished his drink while he eyes me.

"This is strictly off the record? I don't want to get involved in any mess."

"Strictly off the record."

"Mitch Jackson was a drug pusher."

It was common knowledge that the Army, fighting in Vietnam, had a high percentage of drug addicts, and a lot of youngsters were on reefers. All the same this was something I hadn't expected to hear.

"That's a serious accusation, Hank," I said. "If you knew, why didn't you report to Colonel Parnell?"

He gave a sour smile.

"Because I wanted to stay alive. I wasn't the only one who knew, but no report was made. I'll tell you something. A sergeant, working under Jackson, found out what Jackson was up to. He told Jackson to pack it in or he'd put in a report. The sergeant and Jackson went out together on a patrol. The sergeant didn't come back. Jackson reported he had been killed by a 'Nam sniper. A couple of kids, when Jackson propositioned them to buy his junk, refused. They also died by snipers' bullets, so the word got around to keep the mouth shut. Anyway, what good would I've done? I'd only have landed myself in trouble. A coloured man reporting a favourite Staff sergeant to a man like Colonel Parnell who thought Jackson was the tops? So I kept my mouth shut."

It looked now as if the citizens of Searle had been right about Mitch Jackson and Colonel Parnell had been wrong.

"Any idea how Jackson got hold of the drugs?"

"No, and I didn't want to know and I don't want to know now."

"He must have been picking up a lot of money."

"I told you: at least a thousand bucks a week. The kids were really hooked. Some of them had wealthy parents who sent them money. Others stole anything they could lay hands on in Saigon when they were pulled out of the line for a week's rest."

"What did he do with money like that? He couldn't have spent it."

Hank shrugged.

"I wouldn't know. Jackson wasn't the only pusher. There were a lot of them: he was the only one in our outfit, but there were pushers in every outfit. Maybe the pushers pooled the take and got it back home."

I thought that was likely.

"Does the name Syd Watkins mean anything to you?"

Hank thought, then shook his head.

"No. He wasn't in our outfit."

At this moment, Mrs Smith appeared in the doorway.

"You want to eat, Hank? The chicken will fall to bits if you don't."

Taking the hint, I got to my feet.

"Well, thanks, Hank." I shook his hand. "If there's anything else I think of, can I see you again?"

He nodded.

"So long as it's strictly off the record."

As I left, I gave Mrs Smith a friendly smile, but her expression was wooden. From her angle, I wouldn't be welcomed again.

I went down the path and to my car. Even in the darkness, I could feel hundreds of eyes watching me.

As I got into my car, a big, coloured man, wearing a dark, open neck shirt and dark cotton trousers, slouched out of the shadows. He had a pair of shoulders on him that Ali might have envied. He rested two enormous black hands on the windowsill of my car and leaned forward. I could smell gin on his breath.

"We don't like white men in this district," he said in a soft threatening voice. "Piss off, white man, and don't come back."

I started the engine and shifted to "Drive."

"Piss off yourself," I said, looking up at him, "and screw you, black boy." I trod down hard on the gas pedal and shot the car away. In the driving mirror, I saw him move into the middle of the street, his fists clenched. He looked like a savage gorilla.

Well, I had learned something. I had learned Mitch Jackson wasn't a white-headed hero. I learned he was the lowest scum on earth. A sonofabitch who sells drugs to kids was just that. I had a lot to think about, but it occurred to me, as I headed back to Paradise City, that I was allowing myself to be sidetracked.

My job was to find Fred Jackson's grandson, yet I had a distinct hunch that Jackson's murder and Mitch Jackson's drug pushing were somehow hooked up with the kid's disappearance. It was just a hunch, but I had confidence in my hunches: they had often paid off when I was working for my father.

It was now too late to drive to Searle, so I headed back to my two-room apartment.

I parked the car in the underground garage and took the elevator to my apartment on the sixth floor.

My mind was busy as I unlocked my door and this accounted for my not paying attention to the fact I had trouble in turning the lock. At any other time, when I wasn't thinking so hard, I would have been alerted.

As I moved into my small, comfortably furnished living-room and turned on the light I smelt them before I saw them. The stink of unwashed bodies hung in the room bringing me to instant alert.

They came out of my bedroom like two black shadows, evil-looking flick-knives in their black hands.

My neighbour below turned on his TV set and a voice began to boom out the news.

3

The sight of these two black men really had me scared. They moved apart at my bedroom door: one moving to the right, the other to the left.

The one on the right was tall, emaciated with sugar-spun hair. He wore a filthy goatskin waistcoat hanging open, showing his skeleton-like chest. Ropes of cheap coloured beads flopped down to his navel. His skin-tight scarlet trousers were stained at the crotch. The one on the left was shorter, but also emaciated. He wore a greasy black sombrero, a tattered leather jerkin and black leather trousers. Both of them were bare footed and their feet were filthy and stank.

All this I took in with one glance.

If it hadn't been for their smell, they would have had me, but when I walked into my room their body-smell saved me.

The front door was still open.

As they came at me, I saw their pupil-less eyes. They were higher than the moon.

I jumped back into the corridor, slammed the front door shut and darted to the elevator which was still standing on my floor. I was in it, thumbing the down button as they tore open my door. The elevator doors swished shut as they dived towards it.

I leaned against the wall of the cage as it sank, aware my breathing was coming in gasps. Man! Was I scared! Those two were the most vicious and lethal-looking muggers I had ever seen.

As the elevator slowly descended, I heard them pounding down the stairs after it. Their naked feet made thudding sounds as they jumped the stairs three at a time. I realized they would outrun the elevator and would be waiting as I came out.

I waited until I heard them thud past the descending elevator, then pressed the stop button. I had reached the 3rd floor. I pressed the button for the 6th floor.

'That'll fox you, you bastards,' I thought as the elevator began to climb. I thought longingly of the .38 revolver in my closet, but I wasn't taking the chance to get back into my apartment and get the gun. They could catch me before I got it.

I felt safe in the elevator's cage.

As the elevator climbed, I heard thumping of bare feet. One of them was chasing the elevator while the other waited below.

That halved the odds, but I had no enthusiasm to grapple with a hopped-up mugger, armed with a flick-knife.

The elevator door swished open on the 6th floor. I was just in time to see Sombrero come tearing around the head of the stairs. I pressed the button to the 14th floor, the top floor. As the doors swished open, he arrived, glaring with murderous hate. He tried to insert his knife between the closing doors, but he was just too late.

Again the elevator began to ascend. I heard him thumping up the stairs. I looked longingly at the alarm button that set off a bell should someone get trapped, but I decided not to touch it. The janitor was elderly and I liked him. Those two thugs would cut him to pieces if he appeared on the scene.

Arriving on the 14th floor, the doors opened. I had my finger on the third-floor button. Although I could hear Sombrero coming up the stairs, I waited, listening to his gasps and snorts.

He was obviously running out of gas. As he came staggering around the corner, I waved to him and pressed the button. The elevator began to descend.

Listening, I couldn't hear him running down the stairs. Thankfully, I decided he was blown.

But there was still Goatskin.

Facing the elevator on the third floor was a good neighbour of mine. If I could get into his apartment, lock the door and call the cops, I could still get out of this nightmare with a whole skin. But suppose he wasn't at home? Suppose he took time to answer my ring? I could get caught by Goatskin as I frantically rang the bell.

As the elevator slowly sank, I stripped off my jacket and bound it around my left arm. That would give me a small protection against a slashing knife.

The elevator doors swished open at the 3rd floor. I sprang out and towards my neighbour's front door.

Goatskin was waiting. I had just time to throw up my jacket-covered arm as he slashed. If it hadn't been for my wallet in my jacket pocket, I would have been cut.

Weaving to my right, I slammed my fist into the side of his face. He had no muscles nor bones. He went down and began making mewing noises, his knife dropping, his filthy hands covering his face.

Then I heard Sombrero coming pounding down the stairs. I snatched up Goatskin's knife and backed away as Sombrero rounded the bend of the stairs and came onto the landing.

His pal was still making mewing noises. Sombrero paused to gape at him, then he saw me.

I showed him the knife.

"Come on, black boy," I said. "I bet I'm better with a sticker than you."

It is never wise to challenge a punk floating high on heroin. He came at me like a charging bull. His knife stabbed at me, but I was already on the move. My Army combat training had taught me all the tricks of knife fighting. His knife missed me by inches and slammed into the concrete wall. The blade snapped off. Dropping the knife I was holding, I hit him with all my weight behind the punch to the side of his jaw. He went down and out like a blown candle flame.

Goatskin was beginning to show signs of life. I went over to him and kicked him very hard on the side of his head. He stopped making mewing noises and gave a reasonable impersonation of a dead duck.

I picked up his knife, got into the elevator and rode up to the 6th floor. I entered my apartment and bolted the door.

Their awful smell hung in the room and I went over to the window and threw it open.

I stood there, breathing in the hot, clean humid air. I couldn't let these two thugs get away. I had to call the police, but I hesitated, remembering I was on a job and wanted to be in Searle early tomorrow morning. I knew I would be held up by police questions and making a charge, but it had to be done.

As I was turning away from the open window, I paused.

A black car had just pulled up outside my apartment high-rise. A man slid out. As he passed under the street lamp, I saw it was the huge black who had spoken to me when I was leaving Hank Smith's villa. There was no mistaking the vast shoulders, the small head and the black clothes.

I turned and ran into my bedroom, snatched open my closet door, found my .38 police special, checked to see it was loaded, then ran back into the living-room and to the window.

The car was still there, but there was no sign of the gorilla. Was he coming up to my apartment? Was he working with those two thugs?

As I watched, I sweated, knowing I could call the cops, but still hesitating. The gun in my hand gave me a lot of confidence. Without the gun, I would already be yelling for a patrol car.

Then I saw him, coming out onto the street. He was dragging the two thugs, one by his arm, the other by his hair. He tossed them into the back seat of his car as if they had been kittens, then he slid into the car and took off.

I walked a little unsteadily to the liquor cabinet, poured Scotch into a glass and drank it, then I sat down abruptly. I had never been so scared in my life and it took some five minutes for the shock to wear off. With an unsteady hand I lit a cigarette, smoked it, got to my feet, then walked into my bedroom. I opened the window, letting out the foul smell, then returned to the living-room and checked to see if any of my things were missing or had been disturbed. Nothing was missing: nothing disturbed. I went into the now ventilated bedroom and checked: nothing missing; nothing disturbed.

That set my nerves jumping.

I would have been much more relaxed to have found that these two thugs were junkies in search of something to sell, but it was unpleasantly clear to me that they had come either to cut me up or even to kill me.

My nerves began now to jump like Mexican beans.

But why?

Was it because I had talked to Hank Smith? I couldn't think of any reason. The gorilla had been waiting to scare me. While he waited, he could have got my address from the licence tag on my car. As I didn't scare, he could have telephoned these two thugs to wait at my apartment and fix me.

Sitting on my bed, I thought back on what Hank Smith had told me: that Mitch Jackson was a drug pusher. Then I thought of Hank Smith. Was he in danger? I thought of his fat, disapproving wife and the photograph of his two kids. I began to sweat again.

When I was talking with him, I had noticed a telephone in his living-room.

Getting to my feet, I got the book and found his number. As I began to dial, I looked at my watch. The time was 23.30. A lot had happened since I had left Searle.

A voice answered the second ring.

"Yeah?" The voice of a coloured man.

"Hank?"

"No. I'm Jerry, Hank's neighbour."

"Can I speak to Hank?"

There was a long pause, then the voice said, "No one's ever going to talk to Hank now. He's dead."

I felt the shock go through me like a punch in the face.

"What are you saying ... dead?"

"I don't know who you are, mister, and I don't care much. I'm here to look after the kids while Mrs Smith is at the hospital, talking to the cops, for all the good that'll do her and the kids."

"What happened?"

"He was hit by some goddamn hit-and-run bastard. He was going to his club, then biffo!"

Slowly, I replaced the receiver. For a long time, I sat staring into space, feeling chills run up my spine. This was

55

turning out to be one hell of a night. Then I pulled myself together. This was something the colonel had to know. Knowing he wouldn't be at the office, I hunted up his home telephone number and dialled.

Mrs Parnell answered. She said the colonel had just left for Washington and wouldn't be back for at least a week.

"Mrs Parnell," I said, "I am Dirk Wallace. I'm one of the colonel's operators. It is important I contact him."

"You will have to wait until he returns," Mrs Parnell said, her voice suddenly snooty. I got the idea she considered the colonel's operators were less than the dust. "The colonel is on State business," and she hung up.

I thought of consulting Chick Barley, but I decided against it. This was my case. I would have been correct to have consulted the colonel, but no one else.

I stripped off, took a shower and went to bed.

I didn't expect to sleep, so I wasn't disappointed.

The Jumping Frog was the only hotel in Searle. It looked from the outside as hospitable as a knuckle-duster, but, climbing the ten creaking steps to the entrance lobby, I became slightly more reassured.

There was a pretty girl with corn-coloured hair behind the reception desk. She gave me a bright smile.

"Hello there, Mr Wallace," she said as I reached her. "Have you come to stay?"

This didn't surprise me. Everyone knew everyone, including strangers, in Searle. Silas Wood must have been talking.

"That's the idea," I said.

"I'm Peggy Wyatt. My dad owns this hotel, but I run it," she told me. "What kind of room do you want, Mr Wallace, or may I call you Dirk? We're all pally in this town."

I eyed her. She had a nice little body. In fact, she had that thing which told me she wouldn't be hard to drag into bed.

"Sure." I gave her my wide, friendly smile. "Room? Well, what have you got?"

"Between you and me, most of the rooms are pretty crummy, but there's the bridal suite: nice double bed." She gave me an up-from-under look. She had long eyelashes, carefully curled. "A little living-room and a bar refrigerator."

"That sounds like my scene."

She told me the cost and, as I was on an expense account, I said it was fine. She pushed the register towards me and I signed in, then she came around the desk.

"I'll show you."

She was wearing the inevitable skin-tight jeans and I followed her tight little bottom to the elevator. We climbed to the first floor. She kept looking at me, smiling. If Searle was supposed to be pally, she certainly was a great advertisement.

Unlocking a door, she showed me the suite. It was comfortable, a little shabby, the small living-room looking onto main street. The bedroom had a vast double bed and there was a tiny bathroom leading off.

"This is great," I said, setting down my suitcase.

She sat on the bed and bounced.

"The springs don't creak," she said and giggled.

Just as I was thinking this was an open invitation, she got up and walked into the sitting-room.

"Have a drink on the house," she said and went to a built-in refrigerator. "Scotch?"

"Only if you'll join me."

"I prefer gin." As she made the drinks, she went on, "You'll like the food here. Don't eat anywhere else. Our cook is really fancy." She handed me the drink, waved hers at me and drank. She sighed, then again smiled at me. "At this time of the day, I need a drink. My dad doesn't approve."

"Every hard-working soul needs a drink at eleven thirty in the morning," I said and sampled the Scotch. It was smooth and good.

"They tell me you are a private eye," she said. "We don't get any excitement in this dump. Is it true you are looking for Johnny Jackson?"

Feeling this might turn into a long session, I sat down and waved her to the other chair.

"I'll just freshen this," she said and waved her little bottom at me as she bent to the refrigerator. I was startled to see her glass was empty. She refilled, then sat down. "Is it right about Johnny Jackson?"

"Yes."

"Wasn't it a terrible thing that old man Jackson shot himself?"

"These things happen."

"Yes, I suppose. Old people haven't much to live for, have they?"

"Some have, some haven't."

She gulped down half her drink.

"I'd hate to be old."

"Well, it comes. Did you know Johnny Jackson?"

"I went to school with him." She gave me a knowing look, then giggled. "I miss him. All the girls were after him, but he didn't care for any of them, except me."

If Johnny Jackson had gone missing six years ago, she would have been around sixteen. Well, if she wasn't kidding me, boys and girls in a hick town like Searle started sex early.

"From what I hear," I said, "Johnny didn't care for girls."

"That's right. That's absolutely right. He was the kind who only went with one girl ... that was me." She finished the drink. "Do you think you'll find him?"

"I don't know. I hope so. That's my job."

She leaned forward, her pretty face now flushed by the gin.

"I want you to. I miss him."

"From what I've been told he went off six years ago. That's a long time for a pretty girl like you to remember a kid and still miss him."

"He was special. He wasn't like the other slobs here. He had brains. I'm willing to bet he's now a big success somewhere, making lots of money." She sighed. "I dream he'll come back and take me away from this god-awful dump." She stared at the empty glass, her face downcast.

"Did he ever talk about leaving?"

She shook her head.

"He never talked about himself. He never talked about his grandpa."

"What did he talk about then?"

Her eyes shifted.

"Well, you know. We were kids. Sometimes he'd talk about love or how tough the world is for kids. I could listen to him for hours." She looked furtively at the refrigerator. "I guess I'll freshen this." She waved her glass.

"Let it rest, Peggy. Gin isn't good for nice little girls: not too much of it."

She made a face at me.

"What makes you think I'm nice?" She got up and poured another slug of gin into her glass. "No one else does in this god-awful dump."

"Why not?"

She was now more than high. She sneered.

"They'll tell you. The only decent kid ever in this gossip-ridden shit-hole was Johnny."

"Did you and Johnny have a thing together?"

"Why don't you say it? I wanted to but Johnny said real love wasn't like that, and that came when marriage came." She tossed off her drink, staggered a little, let the glass slip out of her hand to drop on the carpet, then, looking wildly at me, she said, a sob in her voice, "That's why I want him found! I want him to come back here and marry me! Find him! Hear me!" and, turning, she lurched out of the room and slammed the door behind her.

By the time I had washed and unpacked, it was time for lunch and I was hungry. I went down to the restaurant. There were around a dozen couples, mostly men, already eating. Everyone looked at me as I came in: some of them gave me a smile, others just nodded. I was sure everyone in the big airy room knew I was an operator working for a detective agency and my job was to find old Fred Jackson's grandson. I sat at a table away from the windows.

A smiling old coloured waiter came over and suggested the special.

"It's one of the cook's best, Mr Wallace, sir," he said. "Pot roast."

I said that was fine with me and he shuffled away.

Conscious of eyes still staring at me, I concentrated on my folded hands on the table. I supposed, sooner or later, I would cease to be a novelty, but this scrutiny, as if they expected me to draw a gun or produce a rabbit or something, bored me.

I became aware of a tall, sad-faced man standing over me.

"I'm Bob Wyatt, Mr Wallace. My little girl tells me you will be staying with us. It's a great pleasure."

As I shook hands, I looked at his thin white face and dull eyes. He would be around fifty and life hadn't been kind to him.

"If there's anything special you want, just tell Peggy," he said, forcing a ghost of a smile. "Have a nice lunch," and he wandered away.

The pot roast was excellent. I took my time over it, then, a little after 14.00, I walked out into the lobby, not before the remaining diners left in the restaurant had nodded and grinned at me and I had nodded and grinned back.

Peggy was propping herself up at the reception desk. She gave me a bright smile, but I didn't stop. I went into the humid heat and walked across the street to the sheriff's office. I was pretty sure that Sheriff Mason would be imbibing his medicine and with luck Bill Anderson would be on his own.

I found him with his feet on his desk, picking his teeth with a match end. When he saw me, he whipped his feet off the desk and jumped up.

"Hi, Mr Wallace. Glad to see you."

"Call me Dirk," I said, shaking his hand. "Could be you and me will be working together soon," and I told him what the colonel had said.

He looked like a man given a million dollars.

"Why, that's great! Thanks, Dirk. That's truly great!"

"The sheriff not around?" I said, sitting down.

"Not for another three hours."

"Tell me, Bill, what's happening to old Jackson's cabin?"

"Nothing. It's for the birds. Maybe someone will want to buy his land, but that's for his grandson to decide. I guess he must be old Fred's only heir."

"And no one knows where he is?"

He nodded.

"That's the situation. Dr Steed says he'll put an ad in the local paper, announcing Fred's death." He shrugged. "I don't know if that'll do any good, but Dr Steed says we have to go through the motions."

"I want to take a look at the cabin, Bill," I said. "Do you want to come with me?"

"You expect to find something there?"

"I don't know until I've looked."

"You mean right now?"

"Why not, if you're not busy?"

He grinned.

"I sit here day after day without a thing to do. It's driving me nuts. Searle has a crime rate you could put on the head of a pin."

"So ... let's go."

On the drive up to Jackson's cabin, I asked Bill about Peggy Wyatt. I sat by his side in his ancient Chevvy, primed to get as much information out of him as he had to give.

"Peggy? There's a mess." He shook his head. "You know, Dirk, I can't help feeling sorry for her and for her father. He has an incurable cancer and hasn't more than a year to live. If it wasn't for their black staff, the hotel would have folded. Amy, their cook, turns out food that brings in the customers. Bob Wyatt just hangs on. He's never out of pain. Peggy runs the place. I went to school with her. She was a bright kid. When her mother died, she quit school to help her father run the hotel, and from then on she became a wild one."

"When did her mother die?"

"Around six years ago. Peggy was sixteen then."

"That's when Johnny Jackson was supposed to have gone missing."

He gave me a quick glance.

"What has he to do with Peggy?"

"A wild one? Did she get into trouble?"

"I wouldn't say that. She sure got into trouble with herself. This town never misses a trick. She began screwing around. She has a bad reputation, but Bob Wyatt is popular. Everyone here is sorry for him so they give Peggy a cover-up." Again he glanced at me. "What you call a fig-leaf. But recently, the word is out, she's hitting the bottle."

"I've heard she and Johnny were close."

"That's news to me. Johnny wasn't interested in girls. Anyway, Peggy would have been the last girl a guy like Johnny would tie up with. He was a serious kid."

"You knew him at school?"

"Oh, sure. I had no time for him. Okay, he was top of the school, but he was a loner." He began to drive up the narrow lane leading to Jackson's cabin. "He was an odd-bod. Some of the boys wanted to rough him up. I remember there was a gang that decided it was time to give him the treatment. I was one of them. We got him in a corner of the playground. The idea was to smear him with paint." He rubbed his chin. "We had this can of paint and a big brush. He stood quietly, facing us. He made no attempt to run away. He just stood there, looking at us." He shrugged. "I don't know, but it suddenly wasn't fun any more. There was something about him that stopped us dead. We all suddenly lost interest or maybe we felt we were being stupid kids and he was grown-up. I can't explain it. There was this steady, unafraid look in his eyes that put him behind a high wall. We made the usual gang noises, then suddenly we all walked away. From then on, we left him alone."

He swung the car to a standstill outside the cabin.

"Well, here we are," he said and got out of the car.

Together, we walked to the front door and pushed it open. The blowflies had left. There was still the smell of decay. The only sound was the distant croaking of frogs.

"Did you check that old Jackson had a gun licence, Bill?" I asked as I stood looking around.

"Yup. He had a shotgun licence, but not for the Beretta."

"Did you check if Dr Steed had a licence for the Beretta?"

"Yup. He didn't."

"Did you check if anyone in Searle owned a Beretta?"

"Yup. No one in Searle owns or has owned a Beretta."

I nodded approvingly.

"You're doing your homework."

"I want to work for Colonel Parnell."

"At the rate you are going, that's what you'll do. Now, let's take a good look around."

We spent the next hour and a half carefully searching the entire cabin. We came up with nothing: no letters, no bills, no photographs. As I looked into the empty drawers of the old bureau, it seemed to me someone had been here before us and had made a clean sweep of everything. I couldn't accept that old Jackson, who had lived here for years, hadn't kept some letters, some papers.

"Looks like we're too late, Bill," I said.

"That's what it looks like." He was kneeling by the bed, peering under it. "Something here."

Together we shoved the bed aside and found a good-sized hole in the floor, half covered with a wooden lid. I moved aside the lid and stared into the empty hole.

I looked at Bill who was staring over my shoulder.

"Maybe he kept money here," I said. "Did you check if he had a bank account at Searle?"

"Yup. He didn't."

I sat back on my heels.

"He must have made money and he couldn't have spent much. This hole could have been his bank, and someone found it."

Bill nodded.

"Makes sense."

I shrugged and stood up.

"We seem to be getting nowhere fast. I was hoping to find some letters or at least a photograph of Mitch and Johnny. Let's take a look at the old coot's clothes."

I opened the closet. There was only a spare pair of cut-down trousers and a shabby leather jerkin. I tried the pockets, but found nothing but dust.

"Lived rough, didn't he?" I said as I closed the closet door. Bill grunted. He was staring at the opposite wall. The sun had slowly moved around to the back of the cabin and was now lighting the gloomy little room. I followed his gaze and saw the distinct marks of where a picture or a framed photograph had hung. It was only because of the sunlight that we saw it. The mark showed the frame had been around twelve inches long and six inches wide.

I stared as I thought, then I said, "At a guess, that frame contained Mitch's Medal of Honor. Above the old coot's bed: a place of pride. It's a guess, but I bet I'm right."

"If some thief came up here between yesterday and this morning," Bill said, "what would he want with a Medal of Honor? It would have Mitch's name on it."

"Who said some thief? Whoever cleared out the drawers and took that frame was the man who shot Fred Jackson," I said. "No thief would clean out every scrap of paper belonging to Jackson. This was the killer, Bill."

"Yeah."

I moved into the steamy sunshine.

"We'll take a look at the frog pond."

We did and found only frogs. They seemed to know that Fred Jackson was no more for they were sitting in swarms along the bank. As soon as we appeared they vanished into the muddy, weed-covered water.

"That's it," I said, lighting a cigarette. "We'll go back."

As we walked to the Chevvy, I asked, "Will the sheriff worry that you are going around with me, Bill?"

"I fixed that. I told him it would be a good idea if I kept close to you and reported to him. He liked the idea."

"Don't over-report, Bill. Give him the idea I'm getting nowhere. I have a hunch that this is a bigger fig-leaf job than I had first thought."

He looked intrigued.

"What makes you say that?"

"Work it out for yourself," I said as I got in the car. "It'll be good training for you." As he started the engine, I asked, "Did you talk to the mailman about Jackson's correspondence?"

"Not yet. I haven't forgotten, but Josh is difficult to catch. I hope to see him tonight."

"Do that," I said and sat back while he drove me to Searle.

Before leaving Anderson outside the sheriff's office, I asked him where Syd Watkins' father lived.

"Wally Watkins?" He looked surprised. "You want to talk to him?"

"Where do I find him?"

"He has a real nice little house just outside Searle," Anderson told me. "It's the third turning on your left off the highway. You can't miss it. There's no other house up there. Wally comes to the Club three or four times a week. He's popular. He and Kitty, his wife, made a real home of the place. It was a terrible thing for Wally when Kitty died."

"When was that?"

"A couple of years ago. The town talk is she pined away for her son, but you know how the locals talk. Dr Steed said it was pneumonia."

"From what I've heard Syd Watkins was a wild one."

"He was that, but you know what mothers are. Wally had other ideas about his son. He and Syd didn't get on."

Before driving to Wally Watkins' house, I stopped off at the Morgan & Weatherspoon frog factory.

I found Harry Weatherspoon at his desk. He gave me a hard stare as I walked into his office, then he grinned.

"Ah, Mr Wallace! The private eye," he said, sitting back. "You sure conned me with that information-for-writers line."

"Sorry about that, Mr Weatherspoon," I said, approaching his desk. "From past experience, I've learned some people don't care to talk to private eyes."

He nodded.

"No offence taken. I hear you are hoping to find poor old Jackson's grandson."

"This town certainly has a great grapevine."

"It sure does. Nothing happens here without the whole town knowing about it within half an hour."

"I'd like to ask one question, Mr Weatherspoon."

"Well, there's no harm in asking. What is it?"

"Old Jackson supplied you with a weekly consignment of frogs. I'd like to know how much you paid him."

He regarded me, his bright, dark eyes quizzing.

"Why?"

"Johnny Jackson must be his heir. The way old Jackson lived, he was spending very little money, so he must have had money stashed away."

"I suppose so. No harm telling you. Some weeks were fair, some good. Take an average, I paid him around $150 a week."

"How was this money paid to him?"

"Always in cash. I would put the money in an envelope and Abe would give it to Jackson and he would give Abe a receipt."

"So he must have been saving at the rate of $100 a week?"

Weatherspoon shrugged.

"Maybe."

"And this has been going on for years?"

"Jackson has been doing business with our firm for some twenty years. I'd say we paid him, taking into account his best years, some $200 a week."

"In cash … no tax?"

"Cash, yes. I wouldn't know about tax."

"So at a very rough guess, he could have saved a hundred thousand dollars?"

"I wouldn't know. There was his son, Mitch. Maybe, he gave him money."

I thought of the hole under Jackson's bed. That must have been where he hoarded his money. Even if my guess was wrong, there could still be a big sum missing.

"Sad for the old fellow to take his life," Weatherspoon went on, "but he hadn't much to live for. We'll miss him. That is a very fertile farm."

"Thinking of buying it?" I asked casually.

He hesitated, giving me his quizzing look.

"Well, yes. I know of a young active frog-farmer I could rent the farm to if I buy it, but it belongs to the Jackson estate. Until his grandson is found or proved dead, there's nothing I can do about it."

"Nothing?" I looked at him.

"Well, as soon as I heard old Jackson was dead, I thought of buying the farm. I have my attorney working on it." He met my steady stare with slightly shifty eyes. "I have instructed him to advertise for Johnny Jackson. You could be a help, Mr Wallace. If you trace Johnny Jackson, I'll ask you to tell him I'd like to talk to him. Tell him he'll get a reasonable price for the farm."

"Who's your attorney?"

"Howard & Benbolt. Mr Benbolt handles all my business."

"Would you mind if I talked to him?"

"Why should I? What about?"

"I'm looking for Johnny. You tell me Benbolt is looking for Johnny. We could save each other's time by not crossing lines."

"Go ahead. He's in the book."

"Right. Well, thanks, Mr Weatherspoon. Let's hope we find the kid," and, shaking hands, I left.

It took me less than fifteen minutes' driving to reach Wally Watkins' house. Bill Anderson's description was an understatement. The little bungalow was compact, white-washed with a small garden, an immaculate, tiny lawn and standard roses. The roses were exhibition blooms. There was a short, gravel path to the front door with red tiles as an edging. The little place spoke of care and attention and loving hands.

Sitting in a rocker under the deep porch was Wally Watkins, smoking a pipe. He was neat in a white suit and a panama hat.

He watched me get out of the car. He would be around seventy: lean, with a white beard and sun-tanned. To me, he looked like an old pioneer who had worked hard, suffered a little, but had finally reached his haven.

I liked him on sight.

"Mr Watkins?" I said, pausing before him.

"No one else, and you'll be Dirk Wallace, an operator working for Parnell's Agency." He thrust out his hand and laughed. "Don't be surprised. News travels fast in this neck of the woods."

"I've already learned that," I said and shook his hand.

"Excuse me for not getting up. I have a bad knee. Now, before we talk, go into the house and into the kitchen: first door on your left. In the frig you'll find a bottle of good Scotch and a bottle of charge water. You'll find glasses right by the frig. Will you kindly do this?" He gave me a friendly smile. "While you're about it, take a look around. I'd like you to see how I live. Frankly, Mr Wallace, I'm proud of the way I'm keeping our home since I lost Kitty."

So I did exactly that. The little bungalow was perfectly kept as the garden. There was a good-sized living-room and a well-equipped kitchen. I guessed from the two doors there were two bedrooms, but I didn't look further. I made the drinks and came out and sat in another rocker by his side.

"Mr Watkins, you can be more than proud of your home," I said.

"Thank you." He looked happy. "Kitty kept a high standard. She really loved this place and she kept it as I am keeping it." He regarded me. "I wouldn't want her to be unhappy." He took the drink. "I believe dear ones keep close." He lifted his glass in a salute. We drank a little. "So you're looking for Johnny Jackson?"

"Yes. Did you ever meet him?"

"Of course. He was a nice kid: smart. When I say smart, I mean he was good at school, and he was a hell of a worker. Make no mistake about that. Kids, these days, don't know the meaning of work: it's pop and fooling, but

70

Johnny used to ride his cycle five miles to school, work, then cycle back, do Fred's laundry, cook his supper, help with the frogs and keep the place clean. He loved Fred. From what I know, I'll say he even worshipped Fred."

"Then why did he take off?"

Wally stroked his beard and shook his head.

"That's what I keep asking myself. Why did Johnny suddenly vanish?"

"Mr Watkins, do you imagine something happened to him? I mean he got ill and died or had an accident and died and old Jackson didn't report it?"

Wally slopped a little of his drink, muttered to himself, then, taking out a handkerchief, he mopped up the slight spill on his trousers.

"Died? Oh, no. Fred would have reported it. Nothing like that. No, something happened up at that cabin that made Johnny run away. That's what I think."

"What could have happened that bad?"

He rocked in his chair.

"That's what I keep asking myself."

"Suppose, as Johnny grew up, he got tired of living rough. Suppose he decided to quit."

"I told you. He worshipped Fred. He wouldn't have left him."

"But he did."

"That's right."

"You knew Fred pretty well?"

"More than well. At one time we were close friends. When the a'gator got his legs, I used to drive up there with groceries. Mitch was there then. He was a good son to Fred, but a real young hellion to everyone else. When he got drafted, he came to see me. He told me to look after his father – as if I wouldn't have! So I continued to drive up there with groceries, but it wasn't the same. Fred turned nasty. He hated anyone seeing him stumping around on his thighs. I guess that's natural, but it grieved me. Then Johnny arrived. Johnny used to come to my store after school and buy stuff. He said Fred didn't welcome visitors, so I kept away. Both Kitty and I felt the kid would look after Fred, so we left him to it."

"Was Fred married?"

"I think so. I'm talking now of some thirty-five or so years ago. That was when I was just starting my grocery store and Fred was working for a frog-farmer ... before he bought land and started up for himself. Anyway, he quit Searle and was away a couple of years. When he returned, he had made a bit of money and brought Mitch back with him. Mitch was around two years old. Fred told me in confidence the mother had died, giving birth to Mitch. Fred liked boys. He was very proud of Mitch. Although both Kitty and I told him he would have a tough time rearing the baby, he just laughed and said Mitch would have to take his chances, and he certainly did. I remember Fred telling me that if it had been a baby girl he would have got it adopted, but having a son meant a lot to him."

"Did Fred save his money?"

Wally looked surprised.

"I don't know, but I've wondered about that. He was getting well paid for his frogs. I guess he must have saved."

"That's why I want to find Johnny. He seems to be Fred's only heir. There's talk about buying the farm."

Wally nodded.

"Weatherspoon?"

"Yes."

"You've met him?"

"I've met him."

"He came to this town around ten years ago and has been buying property ever since. He bought the frog factory. He bought my grocery store. As soon as poor Bob Wyatt passes on, and it won't be long, the story goes, Weatherspoon will buy the hotel."

"The money comes from the frog factory?"

"I wouldn't know. The factory does well, but it doesn't make that kind of money."

"There's talk, Mr Watkins, that a young girl worked for Fred after Johnny disappeared."

He nodded.

"That'll be old Abe Levi. He claims to have seen her, but Abe drinks too much. There are too many stories floating around in Searle. I don't go along with that one."

"Abe thinks Johnny was still there and the girl was shacking up with him."

"That's the sort of rubbish Abe would think. If he saw anyone up there, it was Johnny. You think about it. No girl would want to stay with a smelly, legless old man who disliked the female sex, wash his clothes and live with frogs." Wally laughed. "Doesn't add up."

I thought he could be right.

"Well, Mr Watkins, I won't keep you," I said. "What you have told me is interesting. I want to think about it, then, if I may, I'll be back with more questions."

"Are you going to Fred's funeral, Mr Wallace?"

"I don't think so. When is it?"

"Tomorrow at eleven. All the town will be there. Searle loves a funeral." He patted his knee. "I'll be there too, knee or not."

"Would it help if I took you in my car?"

"That's real kind. It's all right. Bob Wyatt promised to fetch me." He shook his head. "I guess he'll be the next to go."

I shook hands with him and drove back to Searle.

Peggy Wyatt was behind the reception desk as I walked into the hotel lobby. She gave me a brilliant smile.

"Want your key, Dirk?" she asked.

"Thanks, Peggy, and can you give me an outside line to my room, please? I have some phoning to do."

"Pa's out," she said as she handed me the key. I could smell the gin on her breath. "Suppose I come up in an hour and prove to you how comfortable your bed is?"

I felt sorry for her. She was drunk and, for some reason I didn't know about, frustrated.

"Look, Peggy, you're a little young for me," I said gently, "and lay off the gin."

She flushed and glared.

"You don't know what you're passing up."

"Just fix me an outside line," and, leaving her, I took the elevator to my room.

Ten minutes later, I was talking to Chick Barley.

"Got anything for me yet, Chick?" I asked.

"Not yet. This is going to take a little time."

I detected very faint breathing over the line that told me Peggy was listening in.

"No details, Chick," I said curtly. "I have an audience. Just hurry it up, will you?" and I hung up.

I spent the rest of the evening writing up a report covering my visit with Bill Anderson to Jackson's cabin, the hole under the bed, my talk with Harry Weatherspoon and Wally Watkins. This took me to dinner-time. I locked the report away, then went down to the restaurant. There were only four men, on their own, obviously travelling salesmen who ate and worked at the same time. None of them more than glanced at me.

I ate a good steak with French fries, then returned to my room, turned on the TV set and let it bore me until I was ready for bed.

I locked my door, got into bed and went to sleep.

Wally Watkins was right. Searle certainly loved a funeral.

At 10.30, the church bell began to toll. This was the signal for the citizens to appear on Main Street.

Having had a good breakfast, I had retired to my sitting-room and had sat down at the window to watch the proceedings. Every shop, business premises, the post office, the filling station was closed. The only place open was the sheriff's office.

From my window, I looked down at the mass of people, all wearing black and the kids wearing white. These mourning clothes I guessed were stored away and brought out for anyone's funeral. It was an impressive sight.

The hearse, containing an oak coffin with brass handles, which I assumed contained the remains of Frederick Jackson, headed the procession.

Leading was Sheriff Mason who had obviously taken a very heavy dose of his medicine as he lurched slightly as he walked and held a handkerchief to his eyes. A step or two behind him was Dr Steed, followed by Harry Weatherspoon, Bob Wyatt, Wally Watkins, leaning heavily on a cane, and Silas Wood. Among the crowd I spotted Abe Levi. There were no flowers. I guessed the citizens had considered it was enough to subscribe to this handsome coffin. Maybe they thought that a legless old frog-farmer wouldn't appreciate flowers.

I watched the procession out of sight, then I went down to the hotel lounge.

Peggy was behind the reception desk. She stared at me and this time there was no smile.

"Well, they're putting him away in style," I said.

"I'm not talking to you," she said.

I moved to the counter and rested my elbows on it, looking straight at her.

"You lied to me, Peggy, when you told me you and Johnny were close, didn't you?"

She flushed and glared at me.

"Oh, take off! You bore me!"

"You and the rest of the girls hated Johnny because he ignored you all," I went on. "But you, you wanted to be special so you spread it around among your silly little pals that Johnny was secretly in love with you. I suppose it gave you a status symbol. You even began to believe your lie, but you know, as well as I do, Johnny had as much use for you as he had for the rest of the girls. Grow up, Peggy, and cut out this drinking."

She made a wild swing to slap my face, but I easily caught her wrist.

"Come on, Peggy, grow up."

She broke free, her face crumpled and tears spurted.

"I hate you! Johnny was a sloppy little creep! I like real men! Go to hell!"

She turned and ran into the back office and slammed the door.

I was sorry for her, but I had to know, and now I knew.

Leaving the hotel, I walked across to the sheriff's office where I found Bill Anderson sitting at his desk.

"Hi, Dirk!" he exclaimed "What did you think of our funeral?"

"A big deal. Did you talk to the mailman?"

"I saw him last night. Josh may look dim, but he's got a good memory. He tells me old Fred never got any mail until after Mitch died. The Army sent, by registered mail, Mitch's medal. That's the first thing old Fred ever got from the post office. Then, after that, for the past six years, an envelope arrived for Fred. Josh, who is nosey, tells me it was from Miami. It turned up regularly the first of every month."

"The first of the month was five days ago," I said. "Did the envelope arrive?"

"No. Whoever was writing to Fred must have known he had died."

"Fred died three days ago, Bill," I said. "Whoever was writing to him knew he was going to die."

I left him gaping and, as I was walking back to the hotel, the church bell stopped its dismal tolling. I guessed the funeral was over. There was no sign of Peggy as I took the elevator up to my room. I added to my report that she had been lying about her association with Johnny Jackson and also about the mail Fred Jackson had been receiving every month. I locked the report in my briefcase and went down to lunch.

The restaurant was deserted. I ate cold cuts and a salad. The old coloured waiter told me that as soon as the folks returned from the burial the restaurant would be packed. I hurried over my meal and went up to my room to wait.

I watched all the mourners come down Main Street and disappear into their various homes. I waited a while longer, then went down to my car. By then all the shops were open and all the mourning clothes had vanished. It was business as usual in Searle.

I drove to the cemetery. For a hick town like Searle, the cemetery was impressively large and well kept. It took me some time to find Frederick Jackson's grave. I found it in a far corner among shabby-looking tombstones: not an expensive burial lot.

Lying on the fresh-turned earth was a bunch of red roses: there were two dozen of them: exhibition blooms and the kind of roses I would have liked someone to put on my grave when my time came.

I moved closer and saw a card, attached to a bit of wire. I leaned forward and read what was typewritten on the card:

Rest Now In Peace, Grandpa. Johnny.

4

By driving fast, I arrived at Paradise City a few minutes before 18.00. I was lucky to catch Chick Barley as he was clearing his desk.

"Oh, God!" he exclaimed as I walked into the office we shared. "Look, Dirk, I have a heavy date and she won't wait."

"You have the wrong approach. The more you keep them waiting, the hotter they become. What have you got for me?"

"What do you think we are ... miracle-workers? I've got something, but it doesn't amount to much." He sat down, looked feverishly at his watch, then pulled open one of his desk drawers. "Here, you have it. A report on Syd Watkins. So far there is no evidence that Mitch Jackson ever married nor had a kid, but we're still digging at that. The Army says he was single, but the Army could be wrong."

"Johnny Jackson's birth hasn't been registered?"

"I don't know. We're still digging." He handed me a type-written report. "That's it, old buddy, now I'm off."

"Not yet. Chick, you were a cop, serving under Parnell. What was the drug-addiction situation like in the regiment?"

"For God's sake! What's on your mind? You are supposed to be looking for Jackson's grandson, aren't you?"

"You're wasting time, Chick. What was the drug addiction like in Parnell's regiment?"

He hesitated, then shrugged.

"That's old history, but it was pretty bad. Every regiment out there had this problem. It wasn't my business. We had a narcotic squad working on it: they were professionals."

"Didn't they report about your regiment?"

"I guess so, but it went direct to the colonel. I tell you, it wasn't my business."

"This narcotic squad: who was the boss man?"

"Colonel Jefferson Haverford. He and Colonel Parnell are great buddies."

"Where do I find him?"

Chick stared at me, frowning.

"What's going on in that thing you call your mind? This is ancient history. The colonel wouldn't want it aired. He's proud of his regiment and he has every reason to be proud of it."

"Where do I find Colonel Haverford?"

Chick again looked at his watch.

"He lives right here. You'll find him in the book, but listen, Dirk, watch your step. The colonel won't want you to start digging up ancient history." He got to his feet. "If I don't go now, my date will chop off my jewels," and he was gone.

I lit a cigarette, gave myself a drink from the office bottle and read the brief report concerning the Army career of Sydney Watkins.

From the report, I learned Syd Watkins was drafted. He became a bomb-handler: one of the crew who bombed up aircraft. He spent four years in Vietnam at base, handling bombs and nothing else. His work was satisfactory. He was discharged and was returned to the States with other dischargees. The last address the Army had was a lodging-house in East New York. Then he dropped out of sight. The report stopped there.

The only fact in the report that was of interest was that Watkins and Mitch Jackson were out in Vietnam at the same time.

I put the report in a file, then looked up Colonel Haverford's telephone number. He had an apartment in a condominium on Ocean Boulevard: one of the swank districts of the city.

He answered my call himself.

"Haverford," he said in a deep growling voice.

"This is Dirk Wallace, Colonel," I said. "I work for Colonel Parnell."

"Oh sure. You're the new man. The colonel told me about you. What is it?"

"I have a problem, sir," I said. "Could you give me a few minutes?"

"What do you mean ... a problem?"

"It's a job I'm working on. It seems hooked up with Army drugs. I believe you could steer me right."

"You be here in ten minutes. I have a dinner date at eight," and he hung up.

As Ocean Boulevard was three minutes from the office, I was ringing at Colonel Haverford's front door in seven minutes' time.

A coloured maid led me through a big living-room, comfortably furnished, and out onto the terrace that overlooked the boulevard with its palm-trees, the immaculate sand on which the play-boys and play-girls frolicked and the glittering blue sea.

Haverford was sitting in a sun lounging chair. He got to his feet as I advanced. He was a short, squat, red-faced military type with a close-clipped white moustache and a crew cut. He wore white shorts, a white shirt and sandals.

"Wallace?" He extended his hand.

"Yes, sir," I said.

"Okay, sit down. Scotch?"

"Thank you, sir."

He went to the terrace bar and poured two drinks, filled the tumblers with ice, gave me one and sat down. His steel-grey eyes regarded me.

"What's the problem?"

"I understand, sir, you were in charge of the drug problems in 'Nam," I said.

"Correct."

"The Agency has been hired to find the son of Mitch Jackson and, during the course of my inquiries, I have been told that Mitch Jackson was a drug pusher."

Haverford studied his drink, frowning, then he shrugged.

"I have always thought that, sooner or later, this would happen," he said. "Have you talked to your boss?"

"No, sir. The colonel is in Washington and not available, so I've come to you. Was there any real evidence that Jackson was a drug pusher?"

"Now, look, young man. Mitch Jackson is regarded as a national hero. He won the Medal of Honor. We don't want to smear a man's reputation who saved seventeen young men's lives and died while doing it."

"So he was a drug pusher?"

He hesitated, then nodded.

"Yes. He was about to be arrested, as we had arrested a number of other pushers who are now serving long sentences. My assistant had obtained evidence against Jackson and we had a warrant for his arrest. Then this happened: he went into that jungle and got seventeen kids out and died horribly, burned to a cinder. So I decided to forget it. I hate pushers: they are the lowest scum on earth, but, with Jackson, he had guts. We needed men with guts out there. It would have been a real let down to the public if we revealed that, before he died like a hero, he was the scum of the earth. Colonel Parnell wasn't told. This was a cover-up job and I don't regret it. That's it, young man. I'd advise you to forget it too."

I drank some of his excellent Scotch while I thought.

"This could still remain a fig-leaf job, sir," I said. "By that I mean a cover-up job, but I want to investigate further. Did you know Jackson married and had a son?"

He shook his head.

"According to our records, Jackson was a vicious thug before he joined the Army. His past record was very bad, but when he became a soldier his record was excellent. He too did a great fig-leaf job – as you call it – none of the brass had an idea what he was up to. If it hadn't been for my assistant, Captain Harry Weatherspoon, who was tireless when hunting drug pushers, Jackson would have got away with his very profitable racket."

I sat still, trying to keep my face expressionless.

"Captain Harry Weatherspoon? What happened to him?"

"He quit the Army. I heard he had bought a partnership in some factory: something to do with frogs." He shrugged. "Seemed to me an odd job for a smart narcotic agent." He looked at his watch. "I have to change. My wife flips her lovely lid if I'm late for a party." He got to his feet. "Before you go any further with your investigations, I suggest you talk to your boss. I don't know why it seems so important to find Jackson's son, but I do know raking up Jackson's past will cause disagreeable publicity and a reflection on Parnell's regiment. So ... you talk to him."

We shook hands and I left.

The time was 18.40. I decided to go back to my apartment. On the way, I bought a "take-home" Chinese dinner. I wanted to sit and think, and felt no inclination to go out once I was home.

I had my .38 revolver in my hand as I unlocked my front door. No muggers waited for me. I shut and bolted the door, looked into my bedroom, then, putting the gun back in its holster, I made myself a drink and sat down to collate in my mind what had happened this day. It seemed I was making progress. Tomorrow, I told myself, I would call on Howard & Benbolt, Weatherspoon's attorneys, then I would return to Searle. I wanted to talk to Wally Watkins again, then I wanted to talk to Josh, the mailman, and, of course, I wanted to talk to Harry Weatherspoon.

I had an uneasy, growing suspicion as I sat and sipped my drink that Colonel Parnell would take me off this case if I told him what I had discovered so far. I was glad he was in Washington.

After a late breakfast, I drove over to Miami and found the offices of Howard & Benbolt. They were located on the sixth floor of a smart office block on N.W.36 street.

A fat, grey-haired woman sat behind the reception desk. She regarded me with cool, unfriendly eyes.

"Mr Benbolt," I said, giving her a smile and my card.

She stared at the card, then dropped it as if it would soil her fingers.

"You haven't an appointment, Mr Wallace?"

I said I hadn't an appointment.

"Mr Benbolt usually sees clients by appointment."

I said I wasn't a client. I just wanted a brief word with Mr Benbolt unless, of course, he was heavily engaged.

"This is an inconvenient time, Mr Wallace."

I was rapidly getting bored with this old has-been, but I kept my smile glued on and said I was sincerely sorry about the time. What was a convenient time?

She stared at me, not sure if I was conning her or not, then she switched on the squawk-box and announced: "There is a Mr Wallace from Parnell's Detective Agency wanting to speak to you, Mr Edward."

A hearty voice boomed out of the speaker.

"Send him in, Miss Lacey. Send him in."

She flicked up the switch and pointed to a door. Her expression would have curdled milk.

"Through there, third door on the right."

I thanked her, entered a long corridor, rapped on the third door on the right and was told by the hearty booming voice to come in.

Edward Benbolt was a large, overweight specimen of wealth. He was just over forty years of age: immaculate in a dark business suit. Everything about him from his Cardin shirt, his gold cufflinks, his sleek black hair, his red jowls, the carnation in his buttonhole reeked of wealth and confidence.

"Come in, Mr Wallace," he said, rising from behind an enormous desk and reaching out a hand that felt, as I grasped it, to be made of dough. I decided the only exercise Mr Benbolt took was with a knife and fork. "Sit down. Mr Weatherspoon telephoned me. He said you would look in." He showed his expensively capped teeth in a wide smile. "You may be able to solve our little problem, he tells me. We know all about the Parnell Agency: the best."

I sat down.

"I take it Mr Weatherspoon has told you we are acting for the late Frederick Jackson in the endeavour to find his grandson?" I said.

"Exactly. We're trying to find him too. All rather mysterious, isn't it?" He gave a booming laugh. "Mr Weatherspoon is interested in buying the frog-farm, but we can't negotiate without first finding old Jackson's heir."

"Are you satisfied that Johnny Jackson is Frederick Jackson's heir?"

"There's no doubt about that. I have seen a copy of the will."

"So there was a will?"

"Yes, indeed. Old Jackson left all his property and money to his son, Mitchell, and at his death to his male offspring."

"So that cuts out Mitch's wife?"

"If there was a wife, it certainly would. So far we have no evidence that Mitch married."

"If he didn't and Johnny was illegitimate, would that prevent him claiming old Jackson's estate?"

"No. By using the term 'male offspring' he is covered."

"Who holds the original will?"

"Mr Willis Pollack. He is Searle's local lawyer." Benbolt looked patronizing. "I spoke to him on the telephone. He tells me old Jackson made the will when his son was drafted. Apart from the frog-farm, it appears old Jackson left no money. The farm isn't of great value. Mr Weatherspoon would be prepared to pay five thousand dollars for it: not more."

I decided not to tell this fat, smiling attorney about the hole under old Jackson's bed. I was pretty sure there had been a considerable amount of money hidden there, but there was no point, until I investigated further, in telling Benbolt. I could be wrong.

"And you, Mr Wallace. Are you making progress?"

"Not yet. Johnny went missing sometime ago. The trail is cold, but I'm digging. I have only been on the job a few

86

days. I just wanted to meet you and to make sure we don't waste time and money following the same avenues."

He seemed to like that for he nodded approvingly.

"We are advertising. We have contacted the Missing Persons Bureau. As you say it's early days." He glanced at his gold Omega. "Well, Mr Wallace, suppose we keep in touch, huh?" He rose to his feet and offered his dough-like hand.

I shook his hand, said I would keep in touch and, if he had any answers from his advertisement, would he let me know, and I gave him my business card.

I left him, satisfied that I had got more information out of him that he had out of me.

Three hours later, I was in the restaurant of *The Jumping Frog* hotel. Bob Wyatt was behind the reception desk as I walked through the lobby. He gave me a friendly nod. I didn't pause to ask where his daughter was. I sat at my corner table, nodded and exchanged grins with the other diners and ate a good Maryland chicken. When I had finished eating, I asked the old coloured waiter, who told me his name was Abraham, where I could find Willis Pollack, Searle's lawyer. He gave me directions. After coffee, I walked across Main Street, aware I was being watched by curious eyes, to Willis Pollack's office, which was above a hardware store.

It was like entering a 1800 movie set. A little old lady with snow-white hair, wearing a black dress that a costume museum would be proud to exhibit, sat behind a tiny desk on which was probably one of the first Remington typewriters to come off the assembly line. The large room was lined with old-fashioned deed-boxes. By the window was a larger desk and behind it sat Willis Pollack.

I paused in the doorway and regarded him.

Willis Pollack was a tiny man, in his eighties, and he looked like a miniature Buffalo Bill. He had white moustaches, a neatly trimmed goatee, a long hawk-like nose and alert brown eyes. He wore a black frock coat, a white shirt and a gambler's string tie. He looked as if he had stepped out of the past century.

"Ah! It is Mr Wallace," he said. "Come in, friend." He rose to his tiny height, a warm smile on his wrinkled, weather-beaten face. "That's my dear wife, Daisy," he went on. "She does all the work while I do the talking."

The little old lady simpered.

"Now, Willy." She looked at me. "My dear husband always exaggerates. I just don't know what the folks here would do without him."

A little dazed, I advanced into the dim room and shook Pollack's hand, then I went over to Daisy and shook her hand.

Pollack waved me to an old leather-padded chair by his desk.

"In what way can I be of service?" he asked.

I sat down.

"As you know, Mr Pollack, I am trying to find Johnny Jackson," I said. I went on to tell him about the letter old Jackson had sent to my Agency and that Colonel Parnell had accepted the hundred-dollar retainer and, because Mitch Jackson was a national hero, he had instructed me to investigate. "I have talked to Mr Benbolt who tells me Frederick Jackson made a will and you have it. I would like to know when and how the will was made."

Pollack looked over at his wife.

"Show him the will, dear Daisy," he said.

She went to a deed-box and brought me a sheet of paper. There was nothing complicated in the simple statement.

I, Frederick Jackson, leave all my property and my money to my son, Mitchell Jackson. Should he not survive me, then all my property and money is to go to his male offspring whether they are born in wedlock or not. In the event of there being no male offsprings, then my money and property is to go to the Disabled Veterans Fund to help those who are as legless as I am.

Under the scrawling signature which was hard to decipher, Willis and Daisy Pollack had acted as witnesses.

"In wedlock or not?" I said, looking at Pollack. "An odd phrase."

He smoothed his moustache and smiled.

"Not really. Fred knew his son was not the marrying type. He foresaw the possibility that Mitch would have illegitimate sons. Fred had no time for girls. He was odd about this. He told me flatly that no girl would get his money, then when Johnny turned up, I believe for the first time since Mitch left, old Fred was happy."

"What happened about the will?"

"As soon as Mitch was drafted into the Army, I got word from Fred asking me and Daisy to go up to his cabin as he wanted to make a will. We went up there." He shook his head. "For many years, Fred and I had been good friends. We played a lot of snooker together, but when he lost his legs he became a recluse. Daisy and I were dreadfully shocked to find how he was living. The squalor of it! Never mind, he told us exactly how he wanted the will worded. I asked him if he didn't want to make some provision for Mitch's wife, should he marry, and he turned unpleasant, telling me that was his will and that was how it was to be. I wrote it out, he signed it, and Daisy and I witnessed it, and that was that." He fingered his string tie. "I am sure Fred hadn't any money to leave, but only the land and the cabin which aren't worth much so I didn't press him to make a more comprehensive will."

"What makes you think he didn't have any money?" I asked.

Pollack looked a little startled.

"By the way he lived, Mr Wallace. No one would live that rough unless he was short of money. He had no banking account and there was no money found in the cabin after his death."

"Who looked?" I asked.

"Dr Steed and Mr Weatherspoon went up there after Fred died. Dr Steed told me they had a good look around and there were no papers nor money."

"Mr Weatherspoon? Why did he go up there?"

"He wants to buy the property and he and Dr Steed are good friends. Dr Steed thought a witness was the correct procedure when he examined the cabin."

"Didn't they think it odd that old Jackson left no papers?"

"Yes, and so did I, but Dr Steed said he thought that before Fred shot himself he had got rid of all letters and papers."

"Did it seem odd to you that old Jackson shot himself, Mr Wallace?"

"Well, yes. It came as a great shock, but, as Dr Steed said at the inquest, poor Fred led a lonely life and losing Johnny must have been a hard blow. At his age, with no legs, it may have seemed to him the best way out."

I got to my feet.

"So it now remains to find Johnny," I said. "Well, thank you, Mr Pollack, for your time. If I need further help, I hope I can bother you again."

"Don't hesitate, Mr Wallace."

We shook hands, then I shook hands with Daisy and went down the rickety stairs and into the hot street.

This had begun as an unpromising jigsaw puzzle, I thought as I crossed Main Street and walked towards the post office, but bit by bit pieces were falling into place. I was collecting information and that is the heart and guts of an investigation.

Entering the post office, I found a young girl with an acne complexion and wearing pebble glasses, standing behind the wire mesh. She was yawning as I came to rest before her, then obviously recognizing me, she gave me a hopeful smile.

"Hi there, Mr Wallace. Searle's post office is at your service."

"Thanks," I said and, feeling sorry for her drab appearance, I gave her my sexy smile. "Is Josh around?"

"He's sorting the mail." She pointed to a door. "Have you found Johnny yet?"

"Not yet. You'll be the first to know when or if I do."

She giggled.

"I bet. It must be wonderful to be a private eye."

"You can say that again," I said and walked to the door, pushed it open and moved into a tiny sorting office.

A thickset man, balding, in his late fifties, stood at a counter, going through a pile of letters. He had a pipe in his mouth and spectacles at the end of his nose.

"Can you spare a minute?" I asked, closing the door.

He glanced up, nodded and went back to sorting the letters.

"I'm Dirk Wallace. Bill Anderson may have mentioned me. I'm trying to find Johnny Jackson."

He nodded, found a rubber band and snapped it around a dozen or so letters.

"Anderson tells me that on the first of every month you delivered a letter to Fred Jackson. The delivery started soon after Mitch's death," I said. "Every month for six years ... right?"

Again he nodded. So far he hadn't said a word.

"The letters came from Miami?"

Again he nodded.

"Now, no more letters?"

Again he nodded.

"I was told that you took Johnny Jackson when he first arrived in Searle in your mail-van to old Jackson's cabin?"

Again he nodded.

I contained my growing irritation with an effort.

"Did you talk to him when you drove him up to the cabin? Did you ask him where he had come from?"

With maddening slowness, he finished sorting the letters, puffed at his pipe, then, resting two big hands on the counter, he gave me a friendly grin.

"Excuse me, Mr Wallace. I do one thing at a time. I've now done the mail, now I can give you my attention. You're asking about Johnny Jackson?"

I drew in a long slow breath, reminding myself that I was dealing with hick people in a hick town.

"Yes. When you drove him up to old Jackson's cabin, did you ask him where he came from?"

"I certainly did, but the kid just said it was along way. I could see by his tired, white little face he didn't want to talk. Now, Mr Wallace, I respect people's privacy. I don't gossip like other folks in this down do, so I shut up."

"What happened when you took him to the cabin?"

"I didn't. I dropped him at the bottom of the lane. I told him the cabin was right up there and he couldn't miss it." He puffed at his pipe, then scratched his head. "Well, I guess I can tell you this, Mr Wallace. I haven't told anyone else. It's a long time ago and I'd like to help find Johnny." He puffed at his pipe, hesitating.

"Tell me what?" I asked. "Look, Josh, Johnny is old Jackson's heir. You will be doing him a favour to help me find him."

"I guess that's right. Well, he got out of my truck and thanked me: he thanked me real nice. Then he took an envelope out of his pocket. This was some ten years ago, Mr Wallace, but I can see his white anxious face now as he looked up at me. He said he hadn't the money to buy a postage-stamp. He asked me to mail the letter. He said it was important. I told him I would, and I did. The last I ever saw of him was him walking up the lane."

"You mean, when you delivered this envelope addressed to old Jackson each month for six years, you never saw the kid?"

"That's right. I never had the chance. My truck is noisy and Fred could hear me coming. He'd stump to the bend in the lane, take the envelope, grunt at me and that'd be that."

"Did you ever ask how Johnny was getting on?"

"I would have liked to, but Fred never had anything to say. He'd take the envelope and stump off. I was always on my rounds when the kid was at school so I never saw him. Fred didn't even say a thing when I delivered his son's medal. I knew by the way it was packed and the seals it was the medal. He just snatched it from me, signed and stumped off."

"This letter Johnny gave you. I know it was some ten years ago, but do you remember the address on the envelope?"

"Oh, yes. I was curious, you understand. Here was a kid out of the blue, looking for a man as dirty and as sour as old Fred: a kid around nine years of age, so naturally I was curious."

"I see that." I had to control myself not to shout. "What was the address?" Josh found his pipe had gone out. He found a match, struck it, puffed, while I clenched and unclenched my hands.

"The address? The name was Mrs Stella Costa on Macey Street, Secomb. I think it was No. 7 or No. 9."

Had I struck gold? I asked myself. Was this the breakthrough?

"Mrs Stella Costa, 7 or 9 Macey Street, Secomb?"

He nodded.

"That's correct."

"Thanks, Josh," I said, "you've been a big help."

He grinned.

"I liked the kid. If old Fred left any money, I'd like to think the kid has it."

I shook his hand and hurried to my car.

All thoughts of talking to Harry Weatherspoon and Wally Watkins were dismissed. I had to find Mrs Stella Costa, and pronto.

Paradise City has the reputation of being the most expensive, lush-plush city in the world. To keep this reputation, and to cosset the billionaires who live in the city, it is essential to employ a vast Army of workers, street-cleaners, hotel staff and life-guards. This vast Army resided in Secomb, a mile drive from the city.

Secomb is not unlike West Miami: a compact town of walk-up apartment blocks, tatty bungalows, cheap eating-places, tough bars and a number of sleazy nightclubs.

Macey Street led off Seaview Road, which is the heart of Secomb's busy shopping centre.

I was lucky to find a hole in which to park my car. I looked for No. 7 and No. 9. While I looked I was jostled by a steady stream of shoppers: white, black and yellow. Secomb was as active as a kicked-over ant-hill.

No.7 proved to be a small, shabby tailor's shop. The owner, a Chinese, standing in his doorway, gave me a hopeful smile. I moved on. No. 9 looked more promising: a shabby door, sandwiched between a Chinese restaurant and a drug-store.

On this door was a sign that read: *Rooms To Let: Vacancies*. I walked into a dimly lit lobby that smelt of stale cooking, cats and garbage. To my left was a door on which hung a sign: *Rental Office*. I rapped on the door, pushed it open and walked into a small office. At the shabby, chipped desk sat a black man, reading a racing sheet. He was well into his seventies, woolly white hair, dressed in a dark blue aged suit. He wore horn-rimmed spectacles and a small black hat rested on the back of his head.

Laying down the racing sheet, he regarded me and then gave me a sly, inquiring smile.

"What do you fancy for tomorrow's three o'clock, mister?" he asked.

I moved up to the desk.

"I wouldn't know. I'm not a racing man."

He nodded.

"I didn't think you were, but it's always worth a try." He eyed me over, then went on, "And you're not looking for one of my rooms?"

"No. I'm looking for Mrs Stella Costa."

He lifted shaggy eyebrows.

"Now, what should a well-dressed, non-racing young man want with Mrs Costa?"

I gave him a friendly smile.

"She'll tell you if she wants you to know."

He thought about this, taking off his spectacles, then putting them back on.

"She wouldn't give me the time of day."

"That's sad. Where's her room?"

"Mrs Stella Costa?"

I gave him my cop stare.

"I haven't time to waste. Where do I find her?"

"Not here. That's for sure. She moved out years ago." I pulled up a straight-backed chair and sat astride it.

"I didn't get your name."

"Just call me Washington. My dear and departed parents had a sense of humour."

"Well, Mr Washington, can you tell me where she moved to?"

He produced a grubby handkerchief, took off his spectacles and began to polish them.

"We folk in Secomb, mister, have to be careful about giving out information about folk," he said, squinting at me. "I would like to repeat my original question: what should a well-dressed, non-racing young man want with Mrs Costa?"

I had experienced this approach often enough when working for my father. I knew the key that opened the door. I took out my wallet and produced a $20 bill. I figured it, folded it, then looked at him. By this time he had replaced his spectacles. He eyed the bill, then me.

"I see you are an intelligent young man," he said. "A little oil always makes a machine run better."

"Where do I find Mrs Costa?" I asked.

"That's a good question. Where do you find her? I am an honest man, and I would very much like to earn that offering you are showing me, but I believe in giving value for money. Frankly, young man, I don't know where she is, but I can tell you some of her history. Would that interest you?"

I dropped the bill on the desk before him. He regarded it, then picked it up and put it in his waistcoat pocket.

"Now, mister," he said, smiling, "we're in business. You are asking about Mrs Stella Costa?"

"Yes, Mr Washington. What can you tell me about her?"

He held up a pink-black hand.

"Please don't call me Mr Washington. That gives me a superiority complex and, at my age, that is bad for me. Call me Wash, as everyone does around here."

"Okay, Wash. She lived here and she's gone ... right?"

"That is correct."

"How long did she stay here?"

"You want me to start at the beginning?"

"That's the idea."

"Well, then. Some twenty years ago, she came here with her baby son. I don't remember the exact date, but it would be some twenty years ago. From the look of her, I thought she would be about seventeen years of age. She hired my two best rooms. She called herself Stella Costa, but I'm inclined to think that wasn't her real name."

"What makes you think that?"

"As owner of a rooming-house, I have to be a little particular," he said and gave me his sly grin. "When she was out, leaving the baby crying, I looked in just to be sure the baby wasn't making a noise for nothing." Again the sly smile. "I have a pass-key. The baby was just yelling as babies do. There was an envelope in the trash-basket, addressed to Mrs Stella Jackson, so I assumed she was using another name."

"Did she earn a living?"

"Oh yes. She was remarkably pretty and well built. Quite outstanding. She got jobs with various striptease clubs."

"While she worked at the clubs, what happened to the baby?"

"She only worked nights. There was no problem about the baby."

"This went on for how long?"

"Some five years. She always paid the rent. She slept most of the day. In spite of neglect, the baby survived."

"The baby grew up?"

"You can't stop babies growing up, can you?"

"Eventually he went to school?"

"Of course. It may surprise you, but here in Secomb we have a good school. Johnny went there. He was a nice kid: perhaps a little soft, but I was fond of him." He took off his spectacles and polished them again. "It was a pity about his mother."

"What about his mother?"

"Well, Mrs Costa didn't make much money. So she brought men back and Johnny, of course, was in the way. She sent him out to wander the streets until her men friends left. Sometimes, when I wasn't busy, the kid would come to me and I'd give him a bite to eat, but most times I was busy, so he would walk around, often in the rain. He told me that as soon as he could he was leaving home. I didn't take this seriously: kids talk that way, but I should have, I guess. Anyway, when he was around nine years old, he did leave. He was here one day and gone the next. Mrs Costa asked me if I knew where he had gone. I gave her a little lecture about the duties of a mother, but she told me to shut my mouth. She said it was good riddance and she had had enough of Johnny." He rubbed the end of his black nose and shook his head. "She wasn't the maternal type."

"When did she leave here?" I asked.

"About two years after Johnny left. Her last job was at the Skin Club."

I groaned to myself. The gold seam I had thought so promising was petering out.

"She left no forwarding address?"

98

"In my business, I don't forward letters nor do I ask questions. So long as I get the rent, they come and they go."

"Did you ever talk to Johnny about his father?"

"Just once. I wasn't curious, you understand. I was just making talk with the kid while he ate. He told me his father was the best and finest soldier in the Army. I asked him why he thought that, but he just smiled at me and I could see he really thought it was true. He was only seven years old then. You know how kids talk. I thought nothing of it, except to feel sorry for him. I guessed he was a kid of some soldier who had knocked up Mrs Costa. I guess she must have told the kid that his father was the finest and the bravest. I don't know why else he should have been so proud of an unknown father."

It seemed to me I had got all the information I could out of this old man. I had learned a little, but I still had to find Stella Costa.

"Where do I find the Skin Club?" I asked, standing up.

"East side of Secomb Road." He peered at me. "It's run by a Mexican, Edmundo Raiz. Are you planning to talk to him? If you are, keep your hand on your pocket book."

"Thanks, Wash, see you around," I said and left.

The Skin Club was a typical cellar joint that catered for the depraved, the drunks and the randy tourists.

This was the dead time for all nightclubs. The time, by my watch, was 18.05. I paused to look at the fly-blown photographs of strippers, a three-piece black band and a large black woman who leered at me from a fading gilt frame. I descended a long flight of stairs, covered with a tatty red carpet, pushed aside a bead curtain and entered a big room with tables, chairs, a bar at one end and a band dais at the other end.

One solitary light hung over the bar where a man stood staring down at a sheet of paper. He was probably totalling up last night's loot.

This man was dark, swarthy with a pencil-lined moustache and a face that looked as if it had been carved out of stone. He was short, compactly built, with square, powerful shoulders. He lifted his head and gave me a long, steady stare as I crossed the room towards him.

"The bar's closed," he said curtly.

"I don't need a drink," I said, coming to rest at the bar. "I'm Dirk Wallace. I work for Howard & Benbolt, the attorneys. I'm looking for information."

A flicker of interest crossed his face.

"Yeah? What information?"

"We are trying to trace Mrs Stella Costa. I understand she once worked here."

His black eyes narrowed.

"Howard & Benbolt?"

"That's what I said."

"Why do they want to trace her?"

"She's been left a small legacy," I lied. "We want to clear up the estate."

He ran a powerful-looking hand over his sleek hair.

"How small?"

"Small. Not your kind of money, Mr Raiz, but we want it cleared up. Can you tell me where I can find her?"

At this moment a girl came out of a room at the far end, by the band dais. She came across the big room with long, graceful strides. I reacted to her like steel filings react to a magnet. She was around twenty-two, above average height with silky, long, black hair. She wore skin-tight jeans and a skin-tight T-shirt that framed her breasts. She was the sexiest menace to men I had seen for a long time.

Raiz glared at her.

"Piss off, Be-Be," he snarled. "I'm busy."

She came up to the bar and smiled at me. She had sensual red lips and even white teeth.

"Cheapie has to act tough," she said. "Excuse him. He's only just started to wear shoes. Who are you?"

"Dirk Wallace." I eyed her, thinking one night in bed with her would put me in an intensive-care unit, but it would be worth it.

"Hi, Dirk!" She thrust her breasts at me, made a face at Raiz, then she went around the bar and pointed to a bottle of Cutty Sark. "Give Dirk a drink and stop acting like a greaser, Eddy."

"This sex symbol is Be-Be Mansel. She works here and screws everything except elephants," Raiz said. He reached for the bottle and poured three drinks. "Ignore her. Her brains are strictly between her legs."

Be-Be giggled.

"Don't listen to him. Just because he never got there, he's sour." She raised her glass and emptied it in one long, thirsty swallow.

"Will you piss off now, baby?" Raiz said in a soft menacing voice. "This is business."

"I heard. Handsome wants to know where he can find Stella. Why make a thing of it?" she said. "Be your age, Eddy. Tell him."

It happened so quickly, I had no chance to intervene. Moving with the speed of a striking cobra, Raiz hit her with his open hand across her face, sending her crashing back against the rows of bottles, bringing a number of them tumbling down on the floor behind the bar. Then he grabbed hold of her belt, flung her over the bar, sweeping away my drink. She landed on all fours, was up and off like a startled deer to the door by the band dais and disappeared.

Raiz gave me a thin smile as I gaped.

"Forget it, Mr Wallace," he said. "In my trade you have to know how to handle broads. I'll get you another drink." As he poured, he went on, "Stella Costa? That's interesting. She worked for me for a long time. She was my best stripper. That kid, Be-Be, isn't bad, but she hasn't the real touch." He placed the drink before me. "To be tops, a girl has to have just a little extra something."

"I guess." I used some of the drink. "Where do I find Mrs Stella Costa?"

"Yeah." He gave me another of his thin smiles. "Howard & Benbolt? They must be rolling in the green. What's the reward worth?"

"No reward. I told you. We want to clear up the estate. If you must know, she was left three thousand dollars. That would be chick-feed to you, wouldn't it?"

"Who left it to her?"

"I wasn't told. Who cares? Where do I find her?"

His face turned blank.

"I wouldn't know. She quit a year ago. She started to put on weight." He drank, shook his head. "She must have been shoving forty. My clients like them young."

"She just quit?"

"Well, maybe I persuaded her." He produced his thin grin again.

"Didn't she say where she was going?"

He looked bored.

"I didn't ask."

Another goddamn dead end, I thought.

"Well, thanks for your time, Mr Raiz. We'll now have to advertise."

His eyes shifted.

"Who cares about a whore?"

"Was that what she was?"

"Do you have to have it in big print?"

"We'll advertise. Should be a boost for your club. Will Stella Costa, stripper and prostitute who worked at the Skin Club, please get in touch ..." I gave him my knowing smile. "You know the guff."

"You don't mention my club!" There was a sudden snarl in his voice.

"Why not? Lots of tourists would like to know where they can find a stripper, plus a whore. It'd be good for trade, Mr Raiz."

He leaned forward, glaring at me.

"You mention the name of my club and I'll sue!"

"Okay. Then I'll go along to the cop house and ask them. They might come up with more information than you're offering."

"Get the hell out of here!"

"Relax, Mr Raiz. Have another drink. Maybe you do know where I can find her. Give me her address, and I don't advertise nor do I go to the cop house."

He hesitated, then shrugged.

"She's dead. She was drunk and walked into a hit-and-run. You can forget her."

"Come on, Mr Raiz, you can do better than that. I can check that out. Use the thing you call your brain. Where is Stella Costa?"

"Okay, you sonofabitch, you've asked for it," Raiz snarled. "I'm going to teach you a lesson!"

There must have been an alarm button behind the counter. I heard a bell ring distantly. The door by the band dais slammed open and my two old acquaintances,

Goatskin and Sombrero, moved into the room, flick-knives in their hands.

Since my first encounter with them, I carried a gun.

As they moved forward, I did a quick draw. This was one of the many things my father had insisted on that I should learn. I was as good as the best.

The sight of the .38 nestling in my hand brought them to a stop as if they had slammed into a concrete wall.

"Hi, finks," I said. "I'm good at knee-capping. Come on, give it a try."

Out of the corner of my eye, I saw Raiz reached for the bottle of Cutty Sark. As he was about to use it as a club, I hit him across his snarling face with the barrel of the gun. As he folded behind the bar, I smiled at the two blacks who were standing, motionless.

"Fade!" I yelled at them. "Fast!"

They melted out of sight, slamming the door behind them.

Cautiously, I backed out of the room, mounted the stairs backwards, alert for the deadly rush that didn't come. I walked out into the crowded street.

She was there in her T-shirt and skin-tight jeans, waiting. She gave me a tight little smile as she hooked her arm into mine.

"Take me to my pad, handsome," she said, "and let's have an exchange of ideas."

5

"Where?" I asked as we got into my car.

"Straight ahead. Left at the traffic lights. Left again at the next junction." She put her hand to her cheek. "That bastard hurt me."

"Not as much as I hurt him," I said, as I started the engine. "Goodie! I've had it up to here with him. I'm quitting." I drove to the traffic lights, turned left, slowed, then at the first junction turned left again.

"That dump on your right," she said.

By a miracle there was parking-space and I pulled up outside a shabby, five-storey building.

"This it?"

"Yes, handsome. My stinking little pad." She slid out of the car and walked up broken steps to a battered front door. She kicked it open, walked down a dark corridor, fumbled in her bag, found a key, unlocked a door and entered. I kept close behind her.

We entered a tiny room that contained a camp bed, a portable wardrobe, a small table and chair. A dusty, threadbare carpet covered the floor. A door to the left that stood open revealed a toilet and shower.

I closed the door and looked around.

"Is this your home?" I asked.

She went over to the bed and sat on it. It creaked and sagged.

"It's somewhere to sleep." She shrugged. "I spend all my waking hours at the club. Sit down, handsome." She motioned to the chair. "The bed won't hold the weight of both of us, so don't get hopeful ideas."

I sat astride the chair and regarded her.

"Why do you want to find Stella?" she asked.

"I don't. I want to find Johnny Jackson who I think is her son."

She ran a finger along the crease in her jeans.

"What makes you think Stella had a son?"

"Didn't she?"

She gave a giggling little laugh.

"Why do you want to find Johnny Jackson?"

"His grandpa left him a frog farm. Someone wants to buy it. Without Johnny's say-so the farm can't be sold."

"Is it worth much?"

"Enough. Look, honey, don't let's waste too much time. If I find Stella, I could find Johnny and I could relax and forget about this minor deal. Do you know where I can find her?"

She fingered her cheek. A small bruise was now showing.

"I've had it up to here with Eddy. I'm quitting. Suppose you give me a hundred dollars. I need a getaway stake."

"Why should I?"

"I could tell you about Stella and Johnny so you can relax."

I took out my wallet, extracted a $20 bill and offered it.

"What's that for?" But she took it.

"Start talking, honey. The rest will come later if you give me what I want."

"Stella died of an overdose. She had been on heroin for months. That's why Eddy booted her out."

"Eddy told me she had been killed by a hit-and-run."

She nodded.

"He would say that. He's sensitive about drugs."

106

"Stella got her shots from him?"

"I didn't say that, did I?" Her eyes turned cold. "Stella's dead."

"You knew her?"

"Of course. She taught me the stripping trade. I've got her job now."

"Did she tell you Johnny was her son?"

"Yes."

"Did she say who the father was?"

"Another $20 buys the answer to that one."

So I gave her another bill.

"She told me the father was a soldier out in Vietnam."

"Were they married?"

She grimaced.

"Who wants to get married these days?"

"Did she talk about her son?"

"Not often, but every now and then when she was high she did."

"What did she tell you about him?"

"She said he ran away when he was a kid and she was damn' glad he did."

"Did she say why?"

"He was in the way. She had her boyfriends who didn't want a kid around." She nodded to herself. "Made sense to me."

"Did she know where he went?"

"Why should she care? He went, period."

So far, I was getting nowhere fast.

"Did you ever meet Johnny?"

She gave me a bright sly smile.

"You've taken a long time to ask that, and let me tell you, handsome, that's the sixty thousand dollar question."

I had an instinctive hunch that I was going to strike gold. What was fifty dollars to the Agency? I peered into my depleted wallet, found fifty and gave it to her.

"I repeat, did you ever meet Johnny Jackson?"

"Two months ago, the day before Stella died."

"Come on, honey," I said impatiently. "Tell me."

"Give me a cigarette."

I took out my pack, gave her a cigarette, lit it, lit one for myself and waited.

"Well, Stella and I were in the club. We were there alone. It was the dead time. Eddy was in his office. We were talking." She grimaced. "Then these two came in. I've seen fags often enough, but these two were really something to see. One of them was black. He was the bull. The other was his boy: pretty, fair, dressed to make your eyes fall out with beads and bracelets. The black stood at the entrance. The pretty boy came mincing across the room: little steps, hips swaying. I don't have to tell you." She grimaced again. "I hate fags. They spoil the trade. They're everywhere now like a rash of cancer. He came up to our table and simpered at Stella. I thought she was going to spit at him, but instead she just sat like a waxwork. I mean that. She had gone the colour of snow and she scarcely seemed to breathe. 'Hi, Ma,' this abortion said in a high shrill voice. 'I'm short. Lend me fifty, will you?' She just sat there, staring, so I yelled to him to get the hell out. My voice seemed to break the spell. Stella said, 'My God, Johnny! What have you done to yourself?' He grinned at her. 'Come on, Ma! What have *you* done to *yourself*? Give me fifty. I'm short!' Stella started crying, so he reached for her bag and, as he was opening it to help himself, I threw my coke in his face. He started back, screaming 'You've spoilt my clothes!' Then the black came charging across the room. I thought he was going to kill me, but he grabbed hold of Johnny and hustled him out. Stella got up, still crying, and went up to her room. That was the last I saw her alive. She took a treble shot."

The jigsaw pieces were falling into place. Johnny Jackson, the son of Mitch Jackson, drug pusher and a Medal of Honor hero, was a homosexual. This explained why the girls at Searle's school couldn't make an impression on him and also why all those I had talked to had said he was a nice kid, but "soft". I felt, at last, I was getting places.

"Do you know where I can find him?"

"He could be anywhere. No, I don't, and couldn't care less. Look, handsome, I'm taking off so how about the other ten dollars?"

"Where are you going?"

She shrugged, her expression stony.

"I don't know. I've had enough of the Skin Club." She stared at me. "Do you imagine a girl with my looks and my thing will starve?"

"You must be going somewhere."

"That's for sure. New York, maybe. Somewhere where the action is. All I know right now is I want to get away from Eddy. How about the ten dollars?"

"Baby, a hundred won't get you far. New York? That's miles away from here."

She held out her hand.

"Ten bucks, handsome."

"Tell me about Eddy Raiz."

Her eyes widened.

"You crazy? That's one creep I don't talk about. Come on, handsome, I've told you about Johnny, now let's break it up."

"Eddy's in the dope racket," I said. "You don't have to tell me. It's in the big print."

She got up, walked across the room and opened the door.

"Screw the ten dollars ... out!"

I looked at her and felt sorry for her. She was a beautifully built girl, adrift, and struggling to survive as so many kids, her age, are struggling to survive. What had they to offer? Nothing anyone wanted except their beautifully built bodies and their willingness to drop on their backs on a bed. It never crossed their young, stupid minds that the years move on and they would become less and less attractive. Men hunted for the young. Right now, with all the assurance her young body gave her, she couldn't imagine the time would come when some other kid, struggling to survive, would push her down the lust-queue to the waiting perverts and the drunks who would grab anyone in the shape of a woman.

"Honey, pause a moment. Think ahead. You are walking into a mess," I said. "Stella walked into a mess. Isn't there something else you can do except stripping?"

She stared at me for a long moment, her eyes hostile.

"Go shake your goddam tambourine some place else," she said. "If there's one thing I can do well, it's to handle my own life." She pointed to the door. "Beat it!"

I walked away from her, realizing that no talk could influence her, as no talk will ever influence the kids of today unless they want to listen.

As I walked down the sleazy passage to the street, I heard her door slam.

Getting into my car, I drove down the street, turned right, saw a car edging out of a tight parking space. I slammed on my brakes and beat another quester by a whisker. He glared at me as he went on to hunt. I locked my car, then walked fast back to Be-Be's street.

As I walked, I was jostled by the milling crowd. I found a doorway that gave me a clear view of Be-Be's apartment block door. I climbed the three steps, propped myself up against the door post, lit a cigarette and prepared to wait.

Be-Be interested me. I wanted to see where she was going.

After a ten minute wait, the door behind me opened and I glanced around.

A big black buck, wearing an orange shirt and black satin trousers, moved by me. He stank of cheap scent. He took two steps forward, then stopped, turned and stared at me with menacing, bloodshot eyes.

I gave him my cop stare.

"You want something, white man?" he demanded in a gravelly voice.

"If I did, black man," I said, "I wouldn't want it from you." He flexed his impressive muscles that made his shirt strain at the buttons.

"Take the air, white man," he snarled. "Move with the hoofs!"

I undid the middle button of my jacket and slightly opened the jacket, revealing the .38 snug in its holster.

He stared at the gun, then at me, then he gave a weak smile.

"Why didn't you say you were a cop, boss?" he said and moved away, then he set off at a fast pace, shoving his way through the crowd like a bull-dozer shifting heavy soil.

I rebuttoned my jacket, flicked my cigarette butt over the heads of the passing crowd and continued to wait.

Another twenty minutes of patience brought its reward.

Be-Be appeared, looked to right and left, then set off down the street. I expected her to be carrying a suitcase, but she was carrying only a sling bag. I gave her room, then walked after her. She certainly didn't look like someone leaving town.

I had trouble keeping her in sight, weaving my way through the crowd, then abruptly she turned right and for a moment I lost her. I shoved my way past a group of Mexicans who were arguing as only Mexicans can, rounded the corner in time to see her at the far end of the street. She was about to get into a TR7. The car surprised me. It looked new, glittering paintwork: pale blue, an open top. I twisted around a fat woman, laden with shopping-bags, as I heard the little car start up. It shot away, but I was close enough to get the number on the licence plate before she whipped the car around a corner and was gone.

I scribbled the number in my notebook, then walked back to her apartment block. I pushed open the door, walked down the sleazy passage to her door. I expected it to be locked, but it swung open at my touch.

I spent five minutes searching and came up with nothing. The portable wardrobe was empty. The bed sheets were dirty. The shower room, with three fat roaches having fun, looked as if it hadn't been used in months. I came to the conclusion Be-Be had conned me. This sordid room was certainly not her home.

I drove to the office and visited Charles Edwards, the vulture who presided over the expense accounts of all operators. After a short, sharp argument with him, I replenished my wallet, promising to give him a detail statement of how I was spending the Agency's money.

Chick Barley was out. Shutting myself in my office, I called the Traffic Control officer at police headquarters. I had already made my number with him and, as the Agency helped the police, the police helped the Agency.

"Lew," I said when he came on the line. "I want to trace a car registration number: P.C. 400008.

"Hold it."

While I waited, I doodled on a scratchpad, thinking of Be-Be. Why had she taken me to that sordid room? Did she really mean she was quitting the Skin Club? How was it she owned an expensive sports car when she had bitten me for a hundred dollars? Maybe she didn't own the car: borrowed or stolen?

"Dirk?" The traffic controller came on the line. "The car is registered to Mrs Phyllis Stobart. The address is 48, Broadhurst Boulevard. P.C."

"Thanks, Lew," I said and hung up.

I pulled the portable typewriter towards me and typed out my expense statement for Edwards. I hoped it would satisfy him.

The door opened and Chick Barley breezed in.

"You again?" He sat at his desk. "I've something for you." He opened his desk drawer and took out a brief report. "No record of Mitch Jackson getting married, but his son John Jackson's birth was registered by Stella Jackson. Could be the wife, but more likely not." He handed over a photocopy of the birth certificate. It told me no more than what he had already told me. Father: Mitch Jackson. Mother: Stella Jackson. Place of birth: 22, Grove Lane, Miami."

"Well, thanks, Chick. Tell me did you ever come across Captain Harry Weatherspoon, an Army narcotic agent?"

"You still nosing into drugs?"

"Did you?"

"I met him once. He was researching the boys, sorting the goats from the sheep." Chick pulled a face. "I didn't take to him."

"Why was that?

Chick shrugged.

"Envy, I guess. He seemed to have too much money. One of these guys with rich parents. He threw his weight around. You either like a guy or you don't. I didn't."

"Chick, could you get another little job done for me? I want to get back to Searle. I'd like to get the background of a Mrs Phyllis Stobart of 46, Broadhurst Boulevard."

He gaped at me.

"What's she to do with Johnny Jackson?"

"I don't know. Maybe nothing, but I want to know about her just in case."

"Well, Terry hasn't a thing to do right now. I'll get him to dig. How deep?"

"As deep as he can dig."

"Well, okay. And you want it yesterday, of course."

"Tonight will do. I'll phone you from Searle. 21.00 at your place ... right?"

"Not right. At that hour, I hope to be helping a very promising piece of goods out of her dress." He scribbled on a pad, tore off the sheet. "Call Terry. He's still too young to make dates."

"I'll call him." I left the office and dropped my expense account on Edwards' desk. He was talking on the telephone, so I gave him a cheerful wave and bolted for the elevator before he could ask awkward questions.

I got in my car and headed back to Searle.

As I parked outside *The Jumping Frog* hotel, the church clock struck the half hour to 20.00. The drive and my thoughts had made me hungry. I climbed the steps and entered the hotel lobby, expecting to see Peggy at the reception desk, but it was deserted. I crossed the lobby and entered the restaurant. Only five commercials were eating and working.

114

Abraham, the old coloured waiter, beamed as he saw me and pulled out the chair at my table.

"Evening, Mr Wallace," he said as I sat down. "I can recommend the steak stuffed with oysters."

"Sounds fine with me," I said, "and a double Scotch on the rocks." As he noted my order on his pad, I asked, "Where's Miss Peggy?"

He looked at me, his eyes sad.

"Miss Peggy ain't well. She's taking a little rest," and he shuffled off towards the kitchen.

I sat back, lit a cigarette and told my stomach to be patient.

After a ten minute wait, Abraham came shuffling out of the kitchen, carrying a tray. He placed the dish before me and the Scotch on the rocks.

"How's that, Mr Wallace?"

"Looks good enough to eat."

I saw his expression change and a look of fear come into his old eyes. I glanced around.

Harry Weatherspoon was standing in the doorway. We looked at each other, then I gave him a wide smile and a wave. He hesitated for a moment, then came over to my table.

"Hello there, Mr Weatherspoon," I said. "Have dinner on me."

"Thanks, but I've eaten," he said and stared hard at Abraham who ducked his head in a bow and shuffled off.

"Well have a coffee." I said. "I wanted a word with you."

Again he hesitated, then pulled out a chair and sat opposite me.

Abraham came shuffling back.

"Coffee and a brandy," Weatherspoon said curtly. I ate some of the steak.

"Good food here," I said.

"Yes." He was regarding me thoughtfully, on the defensive.

"I hear you're buying the hotel when poor Wyatt passes on."

"There's nothing decided yet."

Abraham brought the coffee and the brandy.

"Put it on my check, Abraham," I said.

He nodded and shuffled away.

I ate some more while Weatherspoon sipped the brandy. He was still regarding me. I let him wait and I could see he was growing impatient.

"How's your investigation going?" he asked abruptly.

"Slow progress. I was talking to Colonel Jefferson Haverford." I looked up sharply, giving him my cop stare.

His eyes flickered, but his face remained expressionless.

"How's the colonel?" he asked.

"You did a snow job with me, didn't you, Mr Weatherspoon? You told me you had never seen Mitch Jackson."

He suddenly relaxed and smiled.

"Well, you did a con job with me, didn't you? That makes us quits."

I reminded myself I was talking to an ex-narcotic agent. I would have to handle him with care if I was going to get worthwhile information from him.

"That's right." I returned his smile. "Colonel Haverford told me you got evidence that Jackson was a drug pusher and you had a warrant for his arrest."

Weatherspoon, putting sugar in his coffee, shrugged.

"Correct. It was a delicate situation. I was just ready to arrest Jackson when he went into his hero's act. Colonel Haverford and I discussed what to do and he decided we should scrub the charge. We have kept this under the wraps for over six years, now you come along and dig it up."

"My job is to find Jackson's son. If I can find him without rattling Jackson's skeleton that's fine with me."

He stared at me, then nodded.

"The kid could be anywhere. I don't envy you your job."

"Your attorney is advertising. Could turn up something."

"I heard you talked to him."

"I'm talking to a lot of people, Mr Weatherspoon. I don't have to tell you: an investigation like this takes time and talk."

He finished his coffee, then sipped the brandy.

"Seems a lot of work to find a kid."

"That's what I'm paid for. After all, you're interested, aren't you?"

"Not any longer. I did think of buying the frog farm, but I've changed my mind." He gave me a shifty look. "I've told Benbolt. I don't want to be bothered and don't want to spend any more money."

"So finding Johnny Jackson now means nothing to you?"

He finished his brandy.

"No." He got to his feet. "Well, I have to be getting along."

"A moment, Mr Weatherspoon. Mitch Jackson must have made a lot of money, pushing drugs. Who supplied him?"

"I don't know." His expression had now turned wooden. "How did you get onto him? What evidence did you collect to warrant an arrest?"

"I don't discuss Army business with a private eye," he said curtly. "Good night," and he walked across the restaurant, out into the lobby and out of my sight.

I signalled to Abraham for coffee. I sat over the coffee for some time, my mind busy, then, leaving a tip for Abraham, I went to the lobby, where there was a callbox.

Bob Wyatt was dozing behind the reception desk. He blinked awake as he saw me.

"You can make your call from your bedroom, Mr Wallace." Bearing in mind that the call would go through the switchboard, I smiled at him and shut myself in the call booth.

I dialled the number Chick had given me. Terry O'Brien answered as if he had been sitting, waiting for the call.

O'Brien was one of the young legmen Colonel employed. He ran errands, did research, hummed like a bee with energy and was so full of ambition he was like to burst.

"Terry? Wallace," I said. "What have you got for me?"

"Hi, Dirk," There were sounds of rustling paper. "Phyllis Stobart? Right?"

"Right," I said, containing my impatience. "What have you got?"

"I've spent the past two hours digging in the Herald's morgue. Fan was a big help, but I haven't come up with much."

Fanny Batley, the coloured night clerk in charge of *The Paradise City Herald*'s morgue, was always helpful. If the Parnell operators wanted to know anything about the citizens of the city, they automatically consulted her.

"So what did you find?"

"Phyllis Stobart, wife of Herbert Stobart. She's around forty, he's around forty-six, give or take. He bought a villa on Broadhurst Boulevard: high class: around a quarter to half a million. This was a year ago. They arrived out of the blue. He claims to have been an import & export merchant in the Far East: Saigon. Sold out before the Viets took over and picked up a bundle of loot. He and she moved in the lower rich strata. From the photos I've seen, he looks a real tough. One of these tycoons who've come up from nothing and throws his money around. She's got more class. I'm judging from the photographs. Their home, and again I'm judging from the photographs, is class. Three cars: a Rolls, and a Jag for him. She has a TR7. Staff of four. He's retired: plays golf and poker. She bridge." He paused, then asked hopefully, "How's that?"

"Fine so far," I said, "but I want to know much more about the woman. I want to know where she came from. Have they any children?"

He gave a suppressed moan.

"Okay. Tomorrow, I'll get onto it. The clippings didn't mention children. In fact, the clippings just gave out on their social life."

"Then get out your sharpest spade and goddamn dig," I said and hung up.

I left the callbox and, seeing Bob Wyatt staring into space, I walked over to him.

"Peggy not well?" I asked, coming to rest before him.

He looked sadly at me.

"She's in hospital."

"I'm sorry to hear that. Is she bad?"

"She has a problem." He shrugged in despair. "They tell me they can fix it." A twinge of pain crossed his pallid face, but he managed a gaunt smile. "Mr Weatherspoon is buying the hotel." He gave another despairing shrug. "He strikes a hard bargain, but I can't manage here much longer. At least Peggy won't starve."

The sight of this thin, sad-looking man in obvious pain depressed me.

"Mr Weatherspoon plans to modernize the hotel," he went on. "The staff will go, except the cook. Well, it's the march of time."

"Mr Weatherspoon seems to be a collector of property in Searle," I said.

He nodded, then reached for my key.

"Are you going to bed now, Mr Wallace?"

I took the key, smiled at him and rode up in the elevator to my room.

I thought over the day, thought about what Terry O'Brien had told me, then, finding I wasn't getting anywhere, I took a shower, got into bed and went to sleep.

I found Wally Watkins cutting dead roses from the bushes that lined the path to his bungalow.

He straightened when he saw my car and came down to the gate to greet me: immaculate in a white suit and wearing a panama hat, he looked as if he had stepped straight out of the pages of *Gone With The Wind*.

"I was wondering when I was going to have the pleasure of seeing you again," he said, shaking hands. "Like some coffee?"

"Thanks, no. I've just had breakfast." The time was 10.05. "How's the knee?"

"It comes and it goes. When it goes, I do a bit of gardening."

I paused to admire the roses.

"Best roses I've seen," I said.

"Well, I talk to them." He laughed. "Flowers respond to talk. They appreciate gentle praise."

We sat in rockers in the shade. He lit a pipe and I a cigarette.

"Well, young fella, have you found Johnny yet?" he asked.

"It'll be a long job. The reason why I've come to bother you, Mr Watkins, is I want to talk about your son."

A shadow crossed his face.

"What has he to do with this?" His voice sharpened.

"I don't know. I'm like a fisherman. I drop hooks into the stream and hope to catch something. Have you heard from him?"

"I haven't heard from him since he was drafted into the Army. That was a good ten years ago, and frankly, I don't want to hear from him. He was nothing but trouble. Kitty would have been alive today if it wasn't for him and the way he behaved."

"I understand that he and Mitch Jackson were buddies."

"A couple of no-gooders. Yes, I believe Syd encouraged Mitch. Syd was bright. Make no mistake about that. He had a head on his shoulders, but he was bad too." Wally removed his pipe, stared at it as he shook his head. "Neither Kitty nor I could figure what went wrong. We gave him all the love we had and that was plenty. He was just bad. Even when he was four years old, he started stealing from my store. He could have had anything he asked for, but it was more fun for him to steal. Later, he got around to stealing from my till. I caught him at it and I walloped him, but it didn't stop him. Then he and Mitch used to go to Paradise City on Mitch's motorbike. Old Fred had given Mitch the machine. They stole there. I knew because I watched Syd and knew he was getting money for cigarettes and clothes from somewhere. So it went on. Kitty never stopped grieving. It killed her eventually."

"Tough," I said. "Didn't he write when he was in Vietnam?"

"He sent Kitty a postcard just once, telling her he had arrived. After that ... nothing."

"Would you have a photograph of him, Mr Watkins?" I said this very casually.

"A photograph? Why, yes. Come to think of it, he did send Kitty a photograph of himself in uniform before he embarked." He looked inquiringly at me. "Want to see it?"

"If it wouldn't be too much trouble." I gave him my wide, frank smile. "Just fishing, you understand."

He thought about this, then got slowly to his feet.

"Come on in. I'll show it to you."

We entered the neat living-room. He went to a drawer and began searching while I moved to the rear window and looked out onto the small back garden. It contained an immaculate little lawn and more rose bushes: these were the long-stemmed blood-red roses you have to pay high for at a florist.

I glanced around the room. On a small desk stood a portable typewriter.

"Do you type, Mr Watkins?"

"My handwriting isn't as good as it should be. I keep in touch with old friends and I respect their eyesight." He straightened, then handed me an envelope. "There's Syd's photograph."

I took from the envelope a quarter-plate glossy: a professional job showing a young man wearing Army tropical kit.

So this was Syd Watkins: narrow-shouldered, close-cut black hair, close-set eyes, an almost lipless mouth, a short blunt nose and a white scar running from his right eye down to his chin. Put him in dirty jeans and a sweatshirt and he was a typical portrait of a vicious thug.

"I never look at it," Wally said, moving away. "He looks what he was, doesn't he? Bad."

"That scar?"

"Oh, that? He got it when he was fifteen. A knife-fight, I guess. Kitty and I didn't ask. He came home bleeding and we fixed him. We were so sick and scared, we just didn't ask." He heaved a sigh. "We learned not to ask questions. It was a waste of time."

I put the photograph back in the envelope and put the envelope on the table.

122

"Have you seen Johnny Jackson recently?" I asked, jumping the question on him.

He stiffened, then stared at me.

"What was that?"

"I asked if you had seen Johnny Jackson since old Fred died?"

His eyes shifted.

"Why do you ask that?"

"Someone put red roses from your garden on old Fred's grave. Someone typed a note that said 'Rest now in peace, Grandpa. Johnny.' The note could have been typed on your typewriter. Did Johnny telephone you, asking you to do this or did he come here and do it himself?"

He fumbled for his pipe, lit it, taking his time. I waited. Then still not looking at me, he forced a pale smile.

"A clever guess, Mr Wallace," he said, "but wrong. I did it. I thought Johnny wherever he is, would like that. It was my idea. Old Fred and I were close friends. I didn't like to think of him being put in the ground without flowers. So I cut the roses and typed the card. Johnny would have done it if he had been here." Again the forced pale smile. "I hope old Fred appreciates what I did, acting for Johnny."

I regarded him. This kindly-looking old man had no guile. It was a good try, but I felt he was lying.

"A nice thought," I said. "So you haven't seen nor heard from Johnny since he disappeared?"

He puffed at his pipe, hesitated, then, still not looking at me, shook his head.

"No, I haven't."

Then I was sure he was lying.

"Well, thanks, Mr Watkins. Maybe, I'll be worrying you again," and, leaving him looking sad and confused, I returned to my car and headed back to Searle.

When I reached the highway, I pulled into a lay-by, cut the car engine, lit a cigarette and went over in my mind the progress report I would have to give Colonel Parnell on his return from Washington. Time was running out. I had only three more days before I submitted the report. I felt pretty sure once Parnell had read my report he would drop the case. For one thing, there was no money in it: for another, my report would expose a fig-leaf job on Mitch Jackson's death. Also Parnell wouldn't want a national hero exposed as a vicious drug pusher, and who cared, anyway, what had happened to Johnny Jackson?

Well, I did!

There were many loose ends that needed tying up and I had to admit to myself I was no nearer to finding Johnny Jackson than when I had begun this investigation.

I remembered my father's advice: *When you are stuck, son, go back to square A, and you might, if you use your brains, find an important lead you have overlooked.*

I was certainly stuck, so I went back to square A.

Frederick Jackson, a frog-farmer, had asked Colonel Parnell to find his grandson, Johnny. He had paid a retainer of one hundred dollars, reminding Parnell that his son, Mitch, the father of Johnny, was a Medal of Honor hero. So Parnell had accepted the assignment, given it to me, asking for action.

I had discovered the following: Fred Jackson had been murdered. To protect a drunken sheriff and to keep the State police from investigating, the coroner, Dr Steed, had given a suicide verdict. There had been a hidden, empty hole under Fred's bed that probably had contained his savings. Someone had cleaned out the cabin, taken away Mitch's Medal of Honor and Fred's savings. Town gossip established that Mitch was a thug who went around with another thug, Syd Watkins, stealing and fighting. Both had been drafted into the Army. An eight-year-old boy had arrived in Searle soon after Mitch went into the Army. The boy was looking for his grandfather, Fred Jackson. The boy, Johnny, had given the mailman a letter addressed to Mrs Stella Costa. The boy remained with his grandfather, attending school until he became fourteen years of age. At this point the news arrived of Mitch's death and his medal award. Johnny had left school and for another six years wasn't seen by the very few people coming to the farm, but Wally Watkins was sure he hadn't left. Then two months ago he did leave since Fred had asked Parnell to find him. For six years, after Mitch's death, Fred had received an envelope, mailed from Miami. Although the Army brass thought a lot of Mitch, a Negro sergeant, Hank Smith, had said Mitch was a drug pusher and he had lost his life while trying to protect his young clients who were his source of income. Smith had been killed by a hit-and-run driver. I had been threatened by a black man, then attacked by two muggers. Then there was Harry Weatherspoon to think about: an ex-narcotic Army agent who was about to arrest Mitch Jackson when Mitch died a hero's death. Weatherspoon had wanted to buy Jackson's frog farm. He had advertised, through his attorney Edward Benbolt, for Johnny, but now had lost interest. Fred's will had been oddly worded; his farm and his money went to Mitch and then, if Mitch died, to go to Mitch's male offspring, in or out of wedlock. So Johnny inherited the farm and Fred's unknown fortune. Stella Costa, apparently Johnny's mother, had worked at a dubious nightclub owned by a Mexican, Edmundo Raiz. A young stripper, Be-Be Mansel, who had replaced Stella when she had left the club, claimed Stella had died of an overdose of drugs, and Johnny, her son, was a homosexual, going around with a black buck. Be-Be used a car registered in the name of Phyllis Stobart, who, a year ago, married a rich, retired merchant from Saigon, Herbert Stobart. Wally Watkins, father of Syd Watkins, had seen Johnny regularly when Johnny came to his grocery store. Wally had told me he had put flowers on old Fred's grave, telling me that it was what Johnny would have wanted, but he was a poor liar and I felt sure Wally was still in touch with Johnny.

I turned all this over in my mind. I didn't come up with anything constructive. There was still a lot of digging to be done. As I was within a mile or so from Fred Jackson's frog farm, and as I had two hours before lunchtime, I decided to take one more look around. It was just possible I might have missed something. A careful search, without Bill Anderson to distract me, just might produce something.

I started the car engine and drove towards the frog farm. Driving up the narrow lane until I came to the wide turnaround, I parked the car and did the rest of the short journey on foot. Rounding the bend, I paused to look at the cabin. The door was ajar. The croaking of frogs blotted out all other sound. There was this eerie atmosphere that I had noticed before: humid heat, croaking frogs, this sinister-looking little cabin.

Automatically, I released the middle button of my jacket so I could get at the .38, snug in its holster. I walked by the well and the wooden tub on trestles where Johnny had washed old Fred's clothes, then, reaching the cabin door, I pushed it open.

For a moment, I stood looking into the dimly lit living-room. Although the sun was strong and hot, it scarcely penetrated the grime-covered windows.

The living-room looked as if it had been hit by vandals. The table was legless, chairs without backs, the dusty carpet thrown aside. Someone had hacked at the walls, making big holes in the wood. The two ancient armchairs had been ripped and revealed the dirty stuffing that oozed out like the entrails of some animal.

I walked into this mess, then into Fred's bedroom. Here again, the place had been ripped apart. His bed, his mattress had all been ripped: stuffing from the mattress made dirty snow on the floor. The closet doors hung open. The back of the closet had had the axe treatment. Fred's dirty clothes were flung into the mess on the floor. The second bedroom was the same: everything ripped, everything axed.

I wiped the sweat off my forehead with the back of my hand as I stared around.

Someone had come, looking for something, and had been determined to find it. The destruction and the mess told me I would be wasting time to look further.

I moved out into the hot sunshine. The almost deafening noise of the frogs made thought impossible.

I decided I would have to tell Sheriff Tim Mason what had happened up here. The destruction could have been done by vandals, but I doubted it. Someone was looking for Fred Jackson's money. The empty hole under the bed hadn't convinced whoever it was that someone else had got the money.

I started towards the lane to my car, then paused. I had a sudden urge to look once more at the frog pond. I had these odd hunches from time to time and this was a strong one.

I walked down the narrow path and as I approached the pond, still hidden by the jungle of trees, bushes and weeds, the noise of the frogs thudded inside my head.

I felt alone and uneasy and I put my sweating hand on the butt of my .38, but it gave me no comfort.

I came silently to the pond.

There seemed to be hundreds of frogs, sitting on the far bank: an Army of them, green, croaking, their little black eyes glittering.

I moved forward slowly, making no sound.

The slimy pond with its thick weeds caught the hot, overhead sun.

There appeared to be some kind of raft in the middle of the pond on which dozens of frogs were sitting.

I moved closer, then I caught my breath as I saw a human hand. This wasn't a raft! It was a body!

I clapped my hands and immediately every frog in sight vanished. I moved down to the edge of the pond and stared at the floating body.

A big bullfrog was sitting on the head of the body. He eyed me evilly, croaked, then leaped into the water.

I stared down at the drowned body of Harry Weatherspoon.

6

From a callbox on the highway, I called the sheriff's office.

Bill Anderson, sounding efficient, answered.

"Bill, I'm reporting that Fred Jackson's cabin has been done over," I said. "I thought you should know."

"Done over?"

"That's right. Taken to pieces."

There was a pause, then he said, "Excuse me, Dirk, but what are you doing up there?"

"I felt lonely. I have a thing about frogs."

Another pause, then he said, "Oh. Well, maybe I had better come up."

"That's why I'm telephoning, and while you're at it, Bill, bring the sheriff, Dr Steed, an ambulance and two husky men in waders."

"What was that?"

"I forgot to mention it, but Harry Weatherspoon is taking a bath in the frog pond. He's very dead, and the frogs seem to resent it," and I hung up.

I went back to the cabin, sat on the bench in the shade and waited.

An hour later, the sheriff's car came up the narrow lane with Bill Anderson driving and Sheriff Mason and Dr Steed seated at the back. The car was followed by an ambulance, containing the two coloured men I had seen before, and two big white men, wearing dungarees and waders.

I walked over to them as they all got out of their cars.

Sheriff Mason was a little unsteady on his legs and stank of Scotch. Dr Steed looked a little older, if that was possible, and worried. Bill Anderson was pop-eyed.

"Take a look in there first, gentlemen," I said and waved to the cabin. "Mr Weatherspoon is in no hurry."

Looking suspiciously at me, the sheriff and Dr Steed entered the cabin.

"Better take a look, Bill," I said. "It's a nice piece of destruction."

He joined the other two.

One of the coloured ambulance men looked hopefully at me.

"We got another customer?"

"That's right. He'll be wet, so, if you have a mackintosh sheet, bring it along."

The three men came out of the cabin.

"Tch! Tch!" Dr Steed said. "Vandals! Kids these, days! They've no respect for anyone's property!"

"What do you think, Sheriff?" I asked.

Mason blinked, then nodded his head.

"Yeah ... vandals."

"Doesn't it look as if someone came up here looking for something?"

"Vandals," he repeated.

"What's this about Mr Weatherspoon?" Dr Steed demanded. "Are you saying he is dead?"

"I would say so, but you might think he's just fooling." I turned to one of the men in waders. "You'll need a grappling hook."

He gave a wide grin.

"Got one," and he produced a long boat hook from the ambulance. The other man in waders produced a big mackintosh sheet. At least, Bill Anderson had been efficient.

I led the way.

Sheriff Mason had difficulty walking along the narrow path to the pond. One of the men in waders had to help him.

The frogs were back, using Harry Weatherspoon as a raft. They all vanished into the pond, as we arrived.

I moved into the shade and propped myself up against a tree while the rest stood around, gaping.

Finally Dr Steed said, "Poor fella. Terrible! All right, boys, get him out."

The ambulance men spread the sheet and the two men in waders moved into the pond and with the boat hook drew Weatherspoon's body towards them. They got him up onto the sheet, then stood back, looking mournful.

I looked at the body from where I was standing. Weatherspoon's mouth and nostrils were clogged with green weed. In his right hand, he clutched a blond, hairy object that was wrapped around his wrist.

"Jesus, Larry!" The sheriff gasped, moving forward and staring down at Weatherspoon. "What happened?"

"Give me a couple of minutes, Tim," Dr Steed said calmly. He knelt and examined Weatherspoon's head, then he sat back on his heels, stared around, then nodded.

"Accidental death, Tim," he said. "It's as plain as the nose on your face." Since the sheriff's nose resembled a large, overripe tomato, I thought this was a tactless remark. I moved over to join Dr Steed.

"What's that he's clutching?" I said, knelt, took the blond object and gently disentangled it while Dr Steed stared, watching me. "It's a goddamn wig!" I exclaimed, shaking the wet blond tresses and holding the wig up so the hair fell straight.

And a wig it was: a cheap wig, sewn on net: the kind of wig you can buy at any self-service store.

"Never mind that," Dr Steed said. "The poor fella is dead."

The sheriff lumbered closer. "Sure it's an accident, Larry?"

"Certainly. Look over there." Dr Steed pointed to a tree with bare roots that crawled down into the lake. "There's a bad bruise at the back of the poor fella's head. He must have slipped, hit his head on one of those roots and he drowned. Oh yes, it's accidental death all right."

The sheriff heaved a sigh of relief.

"No State police, huh?"

"Not for accidental death," Dr Steed said firmly and stood up. "All right, boys, take the poor fella to the mortuary. I'll be along in a while."

"Don't rush it," I said. "Better check his pockets."

"We can do that at the mortuary."

"Better have witnesses, Doc." I looked at Anderson. "Check his pockets."

Anderson hesitated, then, as the sheriff said nothing, he knelt beside the body and quickly emptied the pockets: they didn't produce much: a sodden pack of cigarettes, a silver lighter and a wallet that contained two hundred dollars in small bills.

Anderson made a note of the items, then handed them to Dr Steed.

"The wound is consistent to falling and hitting that tree root?" I asked.

Dr Steed nodded.

"No doubt about it."

"Not someone sneaking up behind him and hitting him with blunt end of an axe?"

There was a long pause, then the sheriff said, "You heard what Dr Steed said. Let me tell you, he's been in the business before you were born. I don't want any of your smart remarks. What are you doing here anyway?"

"Looking for Johnny Jackson, Sheriff," I said. "Have you asked yourself what Weatherspoon was doing up here?"

"He was interested in buying the farm," the sheriff said, his eyes shifting. "I guess he came up here for another look around. That's natural, ain't it?"

"Yeah. He came up here with an axe and did have another look."

The sheriff snorted.

"Go away! You have no right to be here. You're a goddamn troublemaker."

"Ask yourself how Weatherspoon got here," I said. "There's no car. Think he walked?" Then turning, I headed back to the cabin, leaving the sheriff and Dr Steed staring uneasily after me.

I reckoned they would be some time wrapping and carrying the body, so, once out of their sight, I broke into a run. Reaching the cabin, I went in. I should have looked for the axe before: it could only have been an axe to have done all this damage. It took me two or three minutes to find it, hidden under the stuffing from the chairs. It was a short-handled axe with a glittering blade. Using my handkerchief, I picked it up by the blade and examined its blunt end that told me nothing. Then I saw a small label on the handle on which was printed: *Property of Morgan & Weatherspoon*. I put the axe where Anderson could see it, then, leaving the cabin, I went around to the back. There, standing in the shade, was a Honda motorcycle. I guessed it belonged to Weatherspoon and explained how he had reached the farm. It seemed clear to me he had come up, armed with the axe, and had systematically taken the interior of the cabin to bits. What was he looking for? Apparently, the only thing he had found was a blond wig.

The wig didn't puzzle me. I remembered Abe Levi telling me he had seen a girl up here with long blond hair. I had been told that Johnny was a homo. I knew some queers have an urge to wear drag. Johnny could have bought the wig in Searle, and, when old Fred had been out of the way, Johnny had worn it and Levi had caught him wearing it.

That explained the mysterious girl. Wally Watkins had been right when he had told me that if Levi had seen a girl up here it could only have been Johnny. The wig also confirmed what Be-Be Mansel had told me when she had said Johnny was a raving queer.

As I started down the narrow lane to my car, a thought dropped into my mind. Maybe Weatherspoon had found more than the wig. Maybe someone watching him had murdered him. Maybe the same killer who had murdered Fred Jackson.

I got in my car and started the engine.

I knew I should drive straight to Miami and give the whole story to the State police. If I did that, I would be off the investigation. It would then be their business. I hesitated, then decided I would keep digging until Colonel Parnell was back, then I would give him all the facts and let him make the decision.

Back in Searle, I pulled up outside the Quick lunch-bar and walked in. It was crowded. Everyone stared at me as I edged my way up to the counter. The buzz of conversation died. The dozen or so men munching looked hopefully at me.

I ordered a chicken-and-ham sandwich and a Danish to take away.

The man behind the counter started putting the food in a sack.

"Bad thing about Mr Weatherspoon," he said.

All the men, munching, leaned forward to listen.

"We come and we go," I said, not surprised the news had already reached Searle. I paid for the sandwiches.

"Excuse me, Mr Wallace," a little man said, his mouth full of food. "I hear you found Mr Weatherspoon."

"Well, if it wasn't him, it was someone wearing his trousers," I said and left.

I drove to the Morgan & Weatherspoon's factory, left the car outside the high gates and walked across the courtyard to the processing-shed. Here I found Abe Levi, eating from a tin of beans. The smell in the shed made my stomach cringe. The five coloured girls were busy at the messy bench, dissecting frogs. They all looked at me with round black eyes. Abe waved.

I sat beside him.

"You like those beans or would you share my lunch?" I asked, opening the paper sack.

"Bread? Not for me," Abe said. "I like beans. I've eaten beans for lunch for the past twenty years, and look at me."

I regarded him, decided the beans hadn't done much for him and began to eat the chicken-and-ham sandwich.

"So the boss fell into the frog pond and drowned himself," Abe said, digging into his can with a spoon.

"Yes. So what happens to the factory?"

"That's one thing that doesn't worry me. I'm about to retire. I've had enough of lifting frog barrels. I have a nice wife, a nice little home and a bit put by, so why should I care what happens to the factory?"

"Was Weatherspoon married?"

A cunning look came into his close-set eyes.

"You looking for information, Mr Wallace."

I said I was.

"Well, twenty bucks will buy you an earful."

Time was running out so I took out my wallet and gave him a five-dollar bill.

"Let me hear what you call an earful."

"You asked if the boss was married ... right?"

"Come on, Abe, don't play hard to get. You'll get your twenty if you come up with anything of interest. Was he married?"

"No, but he played around. He and Peggy Wyatt had it off together. She thought he was going to marry her, but he wasn't the marrying kind, so she took to the bottle."

"Any idea who will inherit the factory?"

"No one, I guess. Weatherspoon was a loner." He ate more beans. "This factory is worth a pile of money. When the boss took over from old man Morgan, he started a line in canned frogs. That, and supplying all the swank restaurants with frog saddles, must have done him a lot of good."

"Canned frogs? I didn't know you canned frogs," I said, suddenly alert. "You freeze frog's legs, but you don't can them."

"You know something, Mr Wallace? Women these days are goddamn lazy. They feed their men out of cans. Not that I have anything against canned food. I live on beans myself."

"So he started a line in canned frogs?"

"My job was to collect the frogs, but over there there's the canning-shed. It's run by a smart coloured girl. She's been at it since the boss took over. She has a couple of coloured girl helpers." He eyed me, then asked, "Want more, Mr Wallace?"

"It'll have to be more if you want the other fifteen," I said.

He finished his can of beans, stared into the empty can, burped, then said, "The boss was a real sonofabitch. I ain't shedding a tear. He was always after the dollar. He was in some kind of racket." He again looked at me. "Why did he go off every Thursday on that Honda of his and come back here with a leather box strapped to his machine? I often saw him go and, when I was unloading, saw him return. Every so often a Mexican used to come up here and they got into a huddle in the boss' office. Some racket."

"This Mexican?"

Abe shrugged.

"A tough-looking greaser with a little moustache. He came here every month. Then there was a guy who came here in a Jag car. I only saw him once. I was fixing the truck, late. I just caught a glimpse of him, but I wondered who he was. It was around nine o'clock. I heard him shouting at the boss."

I handed over another ten dollars.

"What did he say?"

"I don't exactly remember, Mr Wallace. Something about money. He was shouting 'the pay-off', then he quietened down. I wasn't interested, you understand. I was busy fixing my truck."

"This coloured girl in charge of the cannery," I said. "What's her name?"

"Chloe Smith. You thinking of talking to her, Mr Wallace?"

"Why not?"

"Don't offer her money. For a coloured girl she has class."

"Okay, Abe." I parted with another five dollars. "If I think of anything, I'll talk to you again." Leaving him, I walked across to another shed at the far end of the courtyard.

I pushed open a door and entered a long narrow room. By the window was a long bench on which stood a number of empty cans. Facing the windows was a big electric cooking-stove on which stood two small cauldrons and a deep-fry cooker.

In a corner there was a can-sealer with a stack of lids.

A tall coloured girl came out of another room and regarded me. She was a real looker, her skin ebony black, slim, with half-pineapple-shaped breasts. She wore a floral red and white T-shirt and black cotton slacks. Her head was covered with a red and white cotton scarf. She would be, at a guess, in her late twenties.

"Miss Smith?" I said, giving her my wide, friendly smile.

She moved out of the shadows and into the sunlight coming through the windows.

"We are closed," she said in a low, musical voice.

"I wanted to ask you a question or two. I'm Dirk Wallace."

She nodded.

"I don't have to tell you the bad news, Miss Smith. News of any kind travels fast in Searle."

Again she nodded.

"Did you ever meet Johnny Jackson?"

"No."

"I guess you've heard I'm trying to find him."

"I've heard."

"Miss Smith, maybe you can help me. Mr Weatherspoon wanted to buy the Jackson farm. I understand he sold frog saddles to restaurants, but I didn't know he canned frogs."

She stared thoughtfully at me.

"What has that to do with finding Johnny Jackson?"

I gave her my confidential smile.

"I don't know. In my job, I go around and pick up information, and sometimes, but not often, one bit of information jells with another. Did Mr Weatherspoon do a big trade in canned frogs?"

"No. We sell around five hundred cans a month, but Mr Weatherspoon said it was only the beginning. Last month, we sold five hundred and twelve cans so I guess he knew what he was doing."

"Would it bother you to tell me how the frogs are processed?"

She shrugged and pushed back a lock of black hair under the scarf.

"We get the legs from the shed over the way. They are then dipped in batter and quick fried, then canned. All the customer has to do is to empty the can into a dish and put it in the oven for fifteen minutes."

"That all?"

"Well, no. Mr Weatherspoon invented a special sauce to go with the frogs' legs. It is included in the can in a sachet. The ingredients are his patent. It is one of the quick-made sauces: you put the powder in a saucepan, add water, a little milk and white wine and cook it slow for three minutes."

"Sounds tasty," I said. "I'm always on the look-out for an easy-to-make meal, Miss Smith. Would you have a can I could buy and try?"

She shook her head.

"No. Mr Weatherspoon was very particular about that. He always put the sachets in the cans himself and stood over me while I sealed the cans. He had a list of mail-order customers who subscribed for a monthly delivery. The cans went out in a special container."

"I couldn't buy one of these cans at a grocery store?"

"They were only for mail-order customers. Mr Weatherspoon said we hadn't the equipment to supply retailers, but he was hoping, pretty soon, we could expand."

I was beginning to see some daylight.

"Well, thanks, Miss Smith. What's going to happen here?"

She shrugged.

"I don't know. I suppose I'll have to find another job."

"For a pretty, smart girl like you, that shouldn't be hard. Maybe Mr Weatherspoon had someone working with him who might continue the business."

"There was a Mexican who came here a lot, but I don't know if he was working with Mr Weatherspoon. He could have been a customer."

"I think I know him: pencil-lined moustache, short, broad shoulders?"

She nodded and stared thoughtfully at me.

"Is there anything else you want to know? I want to go home."

"I'm sorry to have kept you, Miss Smith. Just one other thing. Where did Mr Weatherspoon live?"

"He had an apartment over the office."

"He wasn't married?"

"No."

"Well, thanks for your time." I gave her my wide, friendly smile and left her.

As I crossed the courtyard, I looked at the office block. Above were four windows of a living quarter.

I drove to *The Jumping Frog* hotel. I found Bob Wyatt sitting behind the reception desk. He looked close to death.

"Sad news," I said, coming to rest in front of him.

He forced a tired smile.

"Man proposes: God disposes."

"You will get someone to buy the hotel. It's not the end of the world."

"I don't care about myself. I'm continually thinking of Peggy."

"How is she getting on?"

140

"They tell me she will be all right. They are giving her some drug." He looked sadly at me. "She's lonely. I can't leave here to visit her."

"Think she would like a visitor? I've a free afternoon. Suppose I take her some flowers and chat her up?"

His face brightened.

"Would you? She seemed to have taken a liking to you, Mr Wallace. I can't ask anyone else. The ladies here don't seem to like her."

"Leave it to me. I'll go right now. Where's the hospital?"

He gave me directions. The hospital was about half a mile outside Searle.

So, armed with some rather tatty-looking flowers and a copy of Judith Kantz's latest bestseller, I found Peggy Wyatt sitting on the balcony of the small hospital, on her own, and gazing at the pine-tree forest.

She gaped at me, then her face lit up.

"Why, Dirk, this is a surprise!"

"How's the girl?" I asked, putting the flowers and the book on the table beside her.

"I'm going to be okay. I've got over it. Dr Vance is sending me home tomorrow."

"Is that right? That's quick."

She laughed.

"I'm not an alcoholic, although I did behave like one. I was lovesick."

I sat beside her.

"That's good news. How's the lovesickness?"

"Two hours ago, the nurse told me he was dead." She looked directly at me. "I couldn't even shed a tear. I must have been out of my skull."

"When I was your age, I also nearly went out of my skull over a girl," I lied. "It took me time to get over it, but get over it I did."

"How's Dad?"

"He'll be better when you get back. Right now, he's having a tough time running the hotel without you."

"I can guess. Poor Dad. He's so brave. I'll be back tomorrow. Will you tell him?"

"You bet."

"So the hotel won't be sold?"

"There must be other buyers beside Weatherspoon."

She nodded.

"I want to get away from Searle. No one likes me here."

"You talk to Willis Pollack. He could find a buyer."

"Yes. Anyway, I will wait until Dad goes." She looked away. "He's going fast." "Peggy, you just might be helpful. The more I look for Johnny Jackson the more complicated my search becomes. Would you feel like telling me about you and Weatherspoon?"

"What has Harry to do with Johnny?" She looked puzzled.

"I don't know." I gave her my usual line. "I'm like a fisherman. I have hooks out, maybe a fish will bite. When did you first meet him?"

"About two years ago. He came to the hotel to talk with Dad about buying it. There was something about him that hooked me." She lifted her hands in despair. "Dirk, girls can be goddamn fools."

"So can men."

"I guess. Well, I fell for Harry. At first, he scarcely noticed me. Then I could see he was taking an interest. One evening, when Dad was feeling bad and had gone to bed, Harry came in. He asked me to show him the best bedroom." She gave a bitter little smile. "Okay, I fell for it. You can guess what happened." She thought, sighed, then smiled at me. "He really turned me on. I had been screwed often enough, but Harry really knew how to do it. He got me going so all I could think about was the next time we could make love. It was too dangerous with Dad around, so he suggested I come to his home. It was only five minutes' walk. He had a nice place above his office. We were together three times a week. I couldn't have enough of him. Then, I sensed he was cooling off. He would drop in for lunch at the restaurant, smile at me and say he had business, so don't come tonight." She closed her eyes, then shrugged. "I was so hot for him, I would give myself a big slug of gin, go to bed and cry myself sick. God! What a fool I was!"

"It happens," I said. "It's happening every minute."

"I guess." She shrugged. "I've got over it. Now, I'm glad. I saw him only once a month, but I still kept drinking."

"Why are you glad, Peggy?"

"There was something about Harry ... it's hard to explain. I think he was in some kind of racket. There were times when we were in bed, the phone would ring and he would go down to the office. This was after the factory had closed. Several times, I heard him shouting as if he was angry and, when he came up, he looked so hard and ... well, cruel. Those times, he would tell me to go. He said he had business, and once, when I protested, he looked horrible. He scared me."

"You can forget him," I said. "He's out of your life."

"That's why I am glad."

"You said you thought he was in some kind of racket. Why did you say that?"

"I'm not exactly an idiot. Why should he get telephone calls around two o'clock in the morning and throw me out, saying it was business? Besides, there was this truck that came around three o'clock in the morning."

"What truck was that, Peggy?" I asked as casually as I could.

She hesitated, then shrugged.

"Well, he's dead now... so what? It happened when I was crazy about him. I guess I was drinking too much. He came to the restaurant on the night we always dated and told me the date was off. Oh Dirk, I had been longing and dreaming of this night. I wanted him to hold me in his arms and screw me until I screamed. I was burning for him." She looked at me. "Why do I tell you this?"

"They say confession is good for the soul," I said and smiled at her.

"God! You'd get information out of an oyster."

From her sudden change of expression, I was scared I was going to lose her confidence.

"This is important to me, Peggy. Tell me about the truck."

She looked at the tatty flowers on the table and picked them up. She fingered the overblown roses and the Sweet Bay magnolias.

"No one has ever given me flowers before."

I controlled my impatience.

"They will," I said. "You're young."

She put the flowers down and began to finger the book.

"Peggy!" I said, sharpening my voice. "Tell me about the truck."

"Okay. When he had given me the night's brush-off, I guess I got good and drunk. Then, lying in bed, I thought, maybe he had found some other girl. I had to find out. I dressed and went over to the factory. It was after midnight. The gates were unlocked. There were lights on in his apartment. I don't expect you can understand, but what

with burning up and the gin I was half out of my mind."
She looked doubtfully at me.

"I understand."

She shrugged.

"I wonder if you do. It's easy to say that. Never mind ..."
She smiled at me. "I often wonder if people ever understand
other people."

"They can try," was all I could think of to say.

"Anyway, I was sure he had some girl up there in his
apartment. I had to see who she was. Drunk as I was, I
hadn't the nerve to burst in on them. By now Harry was
scaring me, although his lovemaking burned me up. I got
behind a row of barrels, stinking of frogs, and I waited. I
had a three-hour wait. I began to lose my high. I suddenly
could see myself, squatting behind smelly barrels, jealously
tearing me to bits, and as the gin died on me I began to
realize what a stupid fool I was and how worthless Harry
was. I was about to go home, when this truck arrived.
There was a tap on the horn and a man got out of the truck
and opened the gates. The truck drove in and the man
closed the gates. It was dark. I could only see his outline.
Then the office door opened and Harry came out. Light
streamed out of the office and I saw a second man get out
of the truck." She gave a little shiver. "Those two really had
me scared. They were niggers. One of them was wearing
beads and a big wide black hat. The other had on a kind of
goatskin jacket. They looked really weird. They followed
Harry into the office. For the next twenty minutes they
carried out small cartons which they stacked into the truck.
They worked fast, but there seemed to be hundreds of
cartons. When there were no more cartons, these two went
back into the office. From where I was hiding, I could see
right into the office. Harry gave them money. Then they got

in the truck and drove off. Harry went down to the gates, closed and locked them, then went up to his apartment. After a while all the lights went off." She picked up the flowers and smelt the magnolias. "I felt pretty stupid. There was no girl and I was locked in. After wandering around, I found a gate at the back. The lock was rusty. I got the gate open and went home."

"Quite a night out," I said.

"That's why I said he was in some kind of racket." She looked at me. "Does it make sense to you, Dirk?"

"Well, he's dead," I said. "Forget it, Peggy. Now, tell me more about yourself."

I spent the next half hour listening to the inevitable and usual doubts and hopes of a teenage girl. I have learned to become a sympathetic listener. I knew she needed to talk about herself and I said the right things at the right moment.

Finally she ran out of steam and she smiled at me.

"I've never talked to anyone the way I've been talking to you," she said. "If I've bored you, I'm sorry."

I grinned at her.

"You're going to be okay, Peggy. You will have trouble ahead of you, but you'll come through. Talk to old Willis Pollack. He'll find you a buyer for the hotel, but in the meantime get back there and help your dad."

"You're the most understanding man I've ever met," she said.

On that note, I left her, my mind full of the information she had given me.

Back at the hotel, I told Bob Wyatt that his daughter was fine and would be back with him the following morning.

This news made him look five years younger.

After a good dinner of clam chowder, I went up to my room and watched a replay of a Western with plenty of action. When it finished, around 22.45, I equipped myself with a powerful flashlight, checked my gun and went down to the lobby.

Old Abraham was fast asleep behind the reception desk. There were two commercials discussing business. Neither of them looked up as I walked into the deserted street. Searle went to bed early.

The sheriff's office was in darkness. The few street lights made pools of faded light; the rest of the street was dark.

Walking fast, and keeping in the shadows, I reached the frog factory. I took a narrow lane around the high walls until I came upon the gate Peggy had told me about. I paused to listen. In the distance, I could hear the hum of traffic on the highway: no other sounds. The stink of frogs lay heavily on the hot, humid air.

I leaned my weight against the gate and it yielded. I moved into the big courtyard. All the buildings, including the office block and Weatherspoon's apartment were in darkness.

The big moon lit the courtyard and made deep shadows.

I crossed over to the office block, mounted the steps and tried the door. I didn't expect it to swing open so I wasn't disappointed. Using my flashlight, I saw there were three locks, top, middle and bottom. This wasn't a door that could be forced open. Moving around the back of the building, I found another door. This too was securely locked.

I stepped back and surveyed the building. There was a sloping roof and a veranda, then the apartment windows, then another sloping roof. I returned to the courtyard. After searching around among the factory sheds, I found a short ladder, lying on its side in the grass. I carried it around to the back of the office block, set it up and got onto the sloping roof. From there, I climbed over the veranda rail. One of the windows was half open. I lifted the latch, paused to listen, then opened the window wide. Using my flashlight, I found myself in a big, well furnished bedroom. The bed was big enough to accept three people comfortably. I imagined Peggy lying on it, offering her nice little body to Weatherspoon. I moved into the room, opened the door, stepped out into a dark corridor, opened another door and looked into a living-room, also well furnished, neat and orderly.

I wasn't interested in Weatherspoon's living-quarters. I wanted to get down to his office.

There were stairs. I stood at the head of them and sent the beam of my flashlight down to a solid-looking door. I descended to the door to find it locked. Again this wasn't a door to be forced open. I knew if I could open it, I would walk into Weatherspoon's office.

Frustrated, I returned to the apartment. Going into the bedroom, I opened the door of the big closet, facing the bed. Weatherspoon's clothes hung in an orderly row. I spent some time going through the pockets of a number of suits, but came up with nothing. I went through the drawers: many shirts, underwear, socks, but nothing of interest to me.

Finally, after half an hour's patient search, I opened a small drawer in his bedside table. This contained a packet of condoms and a key. Hopefully, I went down to the locked door and tried the key. The lock turned and I moved into the office. I went to the big desk behind which Weatherspoon had sat when I had first met him. Every drawer in the desk was locked. I sat in his chair and examined the locks. It would take a professional to open them.

Leaving the desk, I prowled around the office, found a door, opened it and moved into a small room. Facing me was a floor-to-ceiling steel door. Across the door was a steel bar with a padlock. The door had two locks. Short of blasting the door open, there was no hope of opening it without the keys.

I stood and stared at the door.

Well, I told myself, it was a try. There had just been the remote chance that Weatherspoon's security wasn't top-class.

There was no point in staying longer. I would have to approach from another angle: what angle for the moment defeated me.

Then I heard the sound of an approaching car.

I snapped off the flashlight and moved to one of the big windows. I could hear voices. Then the gates to the factory swung open and a truck drove into the courtyard. It was followed by a car that came to rest beside the truck.

The moon was high now and I could see the truck and the car clearly.

From the car, a short, heavily built man got out. I recognized him: Edmundo Raiz. From the truck two men got out: Sombrero and Goatskin.

I moved fast, opening the door to Weatherspoon's apartment, closing it and locking it behind me, then I moved silently up the stairs. I left by the open window, pushed it to, climbed down the ladder and carried it to a clump of bushes where I hid it.

Easing my gun from its holster, I walked silently around the building, pausing as I approached the courtyard. I edged forward, peering around the wall.

Lights were on in the office. I could hear voices. The door to the office stood open. Light streamed into the courtyard. After a long pause, I satisfied myself the three men had entered the office. I moved forward, keeping to the shadows, then, seeing a pile of frog barrels, I got behind them. This must have been the place where Peggy had hidden and, as she had told me, from there I could look directly into the office.

Sombrero was standing by the desk. Raiz and Goatskin had gone into the small inner room. There was a long pause, then Goatskin came into the office and said something to Sombrero, who followed him into the small room.

Raiz came out and went to the desk. He was holding a bunch of keys. Sitting at the desk, he began unlocking the drawers.

Goatskin came out, carrying a number of small cartons. He went out to the truck and shoved the cartons in, then returned as Sombrero came out, also laden with cartons, putting them in the truck.

I watched Raiz. He was going through a pile of papers he had taken from one of the drawers of the desk. His movements were hurried. Every now and then, he put a paper aside.

The other two, working fast, kept piling cartons into the truck. It was a quick, well organized operation.

Raiz opened another drawer. He took from it a folder, examined it, then laid it with the other papers he had put aside. After unlocking more drawers and taking a quick look, he slammed them shut. I decided he had found what he was looking for.

He got to his feet.

I heard him shout, "Come on! Come on! Haven't you finished yet?"

Goatskin mumbled something and went back to the small room again.

This seemed to me to be my one and only chance, as Sombrero followed him. Drawing my gun, I moved out from behind the shelter of the barrels, took six jumps to the back of the truck, snatched up one of the cartons, spun around and was back behind the barrels in less than three seconds. As I crouched down, Goatskin and Sombrero came out, staggering under another load of cartons.

Raiz spent a few moments relocking the desk drawers, then he took out a handkerchief and carefully wiped the drawers and the top of the desk.

Goatskin was closing the canvas back of the truck. Sombrero was already at the driving wheel.

Picking up the folder and the other papers, Raiz turned off the office lights. He came out, closed and locked the door, then moved swiftly to his car.

"Okay, you two," he said. "Let's go."

He backed his car, spun it around and drove away through the gateway. Sombrero drove the truck beyond the gates and stopped. Goatskin closed the gates and I heard him lock them.

I sat behind the smelly frog barrels, clutching the carton and waited. I didn't move until I heard both Raiz's car engine and the truck's engine die away.

Leaving by the small gate, I walked fast to *The Jumping Frog* hotel.

There was only one light on in the lobby. This was above the reception desk. The lobby was deserted. The two commercials had gone to bed. Old Abraham was sleeping peacefully. His hands folded in his lap. I gently shook the old man awake. He opened his heavy-lidded eyes and blinked at me. Then he stiffened to attention, his black face lighting up with a smile.

"Must have dozed off, Mr Wallace. You need something?"

"I want a can-opener," I said.

He blinked.

"What was that again, sir?"

"A can-opener. Have you one?"

"A can-opener?"

"That's what I want." I spoke in a soothing voice. He must have been pushing eighty and had come awake from a heavy sleep, probably dreaming of his past and his grandchildren. "A can-opener."

He rubbed his forehead, closed and opened his eyes, then nodded.

"I'll get you one, Mr Wallace. If you're hungry, I can fix you a meal."

"Just a can-opener."

He got stiffly to his feet, swayed for a moment, then shuffled off to the restaurant. I waited. It took him some five minutes before he returned.

"Cook won't like this, Mr Wallace," he said, handing me a rusty can-opener. "Can you let me have it back breakfast time?"

"You'll get it." I had a twenty-dollar bill ready. "Thanks, Abraham. When do you get to bed?"

"Mr Wyatt likes to keep open all night. He says you never know. Someone might want a bed and that's what a hotel's for." He gaped as I dropped the twenty-dollar bill in front of him. "Why, Mr Wallace, that ain't necessary."

"Good night," I said, patted his shoulder and, leaving him, took the elevator to my room.

Putting on the light, I locked the door, then put the carton on the table. It was a solid box, measuring around eight inches square and four inches deep.

The label on the box read:

A Product from Morgan & Weatherspoon, Searle, Florida.
 Mrs Lucilla Banbury,
   1445, West Drive.
    Los Angeles.

Using my all-purpose pocket-knife, I carefully eased away the tape that sealed the top of the box and levered the top open. In two snug compartments were two shiny-topped cans. Lifting one of them out, I read the well designed label.

FROG SADDLES:
A luxury meal in itself. Follow the directions for a delicious, satisfying quick meal for two.

The cooking directions were the same as those given me by Chloe Smith.

Using the can-opener, I removed the lid and regarded the neatly packed frog legs, golden in batter. They certainly looked good to eat. Using the blade of my knife, I poked around and unearthed a two inch square plastic envelope containing white powder. I fished it out, then, crossing to the bathroom, I washed the envelope clean.

I guessed what the envelope contained, but I had to be sure. I put the envelope in my wallet, collected the can from the table and rather reluctantly emptied its contents into the toilet. I stripped off the label and added that to the floating frog legs, then I flushed the lot down the drain.

Going to the window, I opened it, made sure the street was deserted, then threw the empty can far into the street. Resealing the carton, now containing only one can, I put the carton in my closet.

I may not have found Johnny Jackson, I told myself as I undressed, but at least my day had been far from unprofitable.

I took a shower and went to bed.

7

Harry Meadows, tall, lean and pushing seventy, had at one time been in charge of the Paradise City police laboratory. When the time had come for him to retire, Colonel Parnell had offered him the job of running the Agency's small, well equipped lab. Meadows had jumped at the offer. He had been considered the best pathologist in Florida and was still, in spite of his age, in the upper echelon, often being consulted by his successor at the police lab.

I found Meadows sitting on a high stool examining a slide under a microscope.

I had driven fast from Searle, taking with me the carton containing one can of frog saddles.

"Hi, there, Harry," I said as I breezed in. "I have something for you."

He waved me away, not taking his eyes from the 'scope.

"Harry! This is urgent and important!"

He sighed, spun around on the stool and smiled at me.

"You young people are always in a hurry. What is it?"

I produced the sachet from my wallet and placed it on his bench.

"Will you analyse this, Harry? It's supposed to be a quick sauce to go with frog legs."

"Is that right? Nice idea, if the sauce is any good. I'm partial to frog legs. Where did you get it, Dirk?"

"Could not be sauce, Harry." I moved to the door. "This is a rush job. I'll be in my office. Will you call me?"

He nodded and picked up the sachet.

In my office, I found Chick Barley was out. All the way from Searle, I had put together, in my mind, the report I would submit to the colonel. Sitting down, I began to pound my typewriter. I was halfway through writing the report when Harry rang.

"Come to me, Dirk," he said, his voice sharp.

Leaving the report, I walked down the long corridor to the lab.

"What's all this about?" Harry asked, regarding me, a stern expression in his eyes. "Where did you get this sachet?"

I closed the door and came close to him.

"What is it?"

"Fifty per cent pure heroin: fifty per cent glucose."

"I guess it would be something like that. Would you know the market price?"

"This sachet is worth three hundred dollars."

I did some mental arithmetic. A sachet in a can, two cans in a carton, some five hundred cartons. The truck-load would be worth three hundred thousand dollars. If there was a delivery once a month – I couldn't be sure of that – but, if so, Weatherspoon's turnover would be three million, six hundred thousand a year.

"Are you sure about the price, Harry?"

He nodded.

"This is the real stuff. I get figures from the Drug Enforcement people each month. This sachet is worth three hundred dollars."

"Thanks, Harry. I'm writing a report for the colonel. I can't say more than that. Hold onto the sachet. It'll be evidence," and, leaving him, I rushed back to my office. It took me another half hour to finish the report, then, putting it in an envelope, I took the envelope and the carton containing the single can of frog saddles to Glenda Kerry.

Glenda was the colonel's personal assistant. Tall, dark and good-looking, around thirty years of age, her hair immaculate, her dress severe, she looked what she was: one hundred per cent efficient and a go-getter.

As I entered her office, she was leafing through a file.

"Hi, Glenda!" I put the carton on her desk. "Will you put this in the safe? It's worth a lot of money, and would you add this envelope?"

"What is this? Are you still working on the Jackson case?"

"Of course I'm working on the Jackson case. The colonel told me to work on it, so I'm working on it."

"You are spending a lot of money." Glenda always judged the results by costs. "How far have you got?"

"It's all in the report, but it's for the colonel's eyes only. Big deal, Glenda. Keep your sticky little fingers off it."

She shrugged.

"Where are you going now?"

"All that will be revealed tomorrow when the colonel returns. He is returning tomorrow?"

"So he said. I haven't heard from him since he left for Washington."

"Okay. Just keep that carton and my report securely locked up."

I left her and, as I was starting down the corridor, I saw Terry O'Brien come out of the elevator.

"I've got something for you, Dirk," he said.

We went together to my office.

O'Brien looked as Irish as he was: powerfully built, below average height, a face that looked as if someone had tried to flatten his nose and nearly succeeded, a cheerful grin and sharp, blue eyes.

"What have you got, Terry?"

"Mrs Phyllis Stobart: maiden name Phyllis Lowery, age forty-two," O'Brien told me as I took down on a pad what he was saying. "I called Tyson and he came up with some dope you might find interesting."

Ritchie Tyson ran a small, efficient private detective business in Jacksonville and there were times when we used his services.

I grimaced.

"What did he charge?"

"I beat him down to a hundred dollars." O'Brien looked questioningly at me. "That okay?"

"Depends what he gave you."

"Some forty years ago, so Tyson tells me, Mr & Mrs Charles Lowery, a childless couple, adopted a girl from the local adoption society. Lowery was highly respectable. He ran a prosperous travel agency. The adopted girl, Phyllis, came to them when she was four years old. There was no information about her parents. She had been dumped outside the adoption society offices. It seems the Lowerys picked a wrong 'un. As the girl grew up, she became difficult: not working at school, always after the boys, then began to steal from the self-service stores, got into trouble with the cops and so on. According to Tyson, the Lowerys really tried, but they couldn't cope. The girl became a JD. She had a spell in detention, escaped, was brought back, finally released. By then, she was seventeen years old. She hadn't been back with the Lowerys for more than a week, when she took off. The Lowerys reported her missing to the police and were thankful she had gone. The police went through the usual motions, but didn't find her. Then one night, some ten years ago, the girl turned up at the Lowerys' home. They told Tyson, who was a friend of theirs and just starting his business, that the girl had altered beyond recognition. She was tough, hard, and scared the old couple. She demanded five hundred dollars. They got the idea she was on the run. They gave her the money and she immediately left. I haven't traced her after that. The Lowerys are dead. The next appearance is her marriage to Stobart a year ago."

"So she had been out of circulation for some ten years?"

"I guess that's right."

"That's a hell of a time to drop out of sight." I thought about this. "Terry, I want you to go to Secomb and dig out an agency that supplies strippers for nightclubs. I want a photograph and history of Stella Costa who once worked at the Skin Club. Her address was 9, Macey Street. Your cover story is she has inherited a little money. That usually gets the business. One other thing, keep clear of the Skin Club. Right?"

"Can do, will do," and he took off.

I spent some minutes typing up O'Brien's report and took it along to Glenda.

"More dope for the colonel," I said, "to go with the other stuff."

She leaned back in her chair.

"I've just heard the colonel is detained in Washington. He won't be back until Monday," she said, taking my report.

I beamed at her.

"That's great news. I have another five days," and leaving her, I hurried down to my car.

I drove to Howard & Benbolt's offices. On my way, I stopped off to eat a hamburger and drink a beer. I reached the offices just after 14.30.

158

The fat elderly woman regarded me suspiciously.

"Mr Benbolt," I said.

"Have you an appointment? It's Mr Wallace, isn't it?"

"Yes to the name. No to the appointment. He'll see me."

"Mr Benbolt has only just come back from lunch."

"I've only just had lunch." I smiled at her. "So that makes the two of us. Will you please tell him I'm here?"

She glared, then switched on the squawk-box.

"Mr Wallace of the Parnell Agency is here, Mr Edward," she announced.

"Send him in," Benbolt's hearty voice boomed.

She gave me a stare.

"You know the way, I believe."

"Sure: third door on the right, down the corridor." She didn't deign to answer and began looking at a legal document. I felt sorry for her. She was old, fat and probably unloved. The little power she had, protecting her boss, was dwindling. Soon, she would be sitting in a one-room walk-up with a cat for company.

I found Edward Benbolt behind his desk, looking flushed and overfed. He gave me his professional smile, rose to shake hands, then waved me to a chair.

"Well, now, Mr Wallace," he said as we settled ourselves. "Have you any news?"

"About what?" I asked.

"The last time we met, weren't you looking for Frederick Jackson's grandson?" I could see his pre-lunch drinks had slightly clouded his mind. "That's right, isn't it?"

"The last time we met, Mr Benbolt, *you* were looking for Johnny Jackson. Did you get any answers to your advertisements?"

He pushed a cigar-box towards me.

"Ah, no. We have dropped the search on Mr Weatherspoon's instructions. Out of curiosity, have you found the boy?" He opened the lid of the box. "Have a cigar?"

"I haven't found him yet, but I'm still searching." I waved away the box. "Thank you, no."

He selected a cigar, smelt it, cut the end and lit up.

"A difficult task."

I gave him a few show-off moments to blow rich-smelling smoke, then I said, "You've heard about Mr Weatherspoon?"

He put on an expression an undertaker would have envied.

"Yes, indeed. I heard this morning. Shocking! A man in his prime."

"Well, no one lasts forever. They come and they go," I said, getting out my pack of cigarettes. "I take it you are handling Mr Weatherspoon's estate?"

"Yes."

I waited, but he seemed more interested in his cigar than Weatherspoon.

"There's the frog factory and the grocery store," I said, "then Weatherspoon must have saved money."

Benbolt regarded me.

"I was under the impression you have been hired to find Frederick Jackson's grandson. Now, apparently, you are probing for information about Mr Weatherspoon's estate which has nothing to do with your investigation." He glanced at his watch. "I can give you no more time."

"Have you ever been to Searle, Mr Benbolt?"

"Searle? Certainly not."

"Be patient with me." I gave him my frank, friendly smile. "I have been digging around in Searle, looking for Johnny Jackson, and I have come up with evidence that, if he were alive, could put Weatherspoon in the slammer for at least fifteen years."

He gaped at me.

"What evidence?" he asked.

"Until I have completed the case, reported to Colonel Parnell, who will then hand the case over to the State police, I can't tell you, but I assure you, Mr Benbolt, I am not fooling. I can find out the worth of Weatherspoon's estate if I wait, but time is running short, so I am hoping you will be co-operative."

"Are you telling me Mr Weatherspoon was a criminal?"

"He was the centre of a drug-ring: more than that I can't tell you."

"Good God!" Benbolt let cigar-ash drop on his ample waistcoat. "Drugs?"

"This is in confidence. What's Weatherspoon's estate worth?"

"I'd say half a million. It depends what price the factory and the grocery store fetch. He invested shrewdly through my brokers. Frankly, I was surprised at the amount of money he made from the factory." He put down his cigar. "Drugs! This is dreadful! I suppose you know what you are saying?"

"I have enough evidence on him to have put him away, but there are others involved and I'm still investigating. Who will inherit his estate?"

He picked up his cigar, found it had gone out and relit it.

"I don't understand. How can a frog factory possibly be connected with drugs?"

"It was a clever fig-leaf operation."

He stared.

"What's that mean?"

"The frog factory was Weatherspoon's cover. Who inherits his estate?"

He regarded his cigar for a long minute, hesitated, then shrugged.

"In view of what you have told me, Mr Wallace, and the fact that my client is dead, and to help you with your investigation, I don't think it would be a breach of confidence to tell you what occurred a week ago."

I waited. These attorneys! How they loved words!

"Mr Weatherspoon came to see me," Benbolt went on. "He was not his usual self. He looked ill. He looked like a man who hadn't had much sleep. This was unusual as Mr Weatherspoon always exuded confidence. He told me he was going to retire. This surprised me as he wasn't more than forty-eight, if that. He wanted me to sell all his stock holdings. I pointed out to him that the Dow Jones index was way, way down, but he said he wanted immediate cash. He also instructed me to sell the grocery store at Searle for whatever I could get for it. I am susceptible to atmosphere and I felt my client was under some kind of heavy pressure. I asked him if he planned to put his frog factory on the market. He said, very abruptly, he would handle that himself." Benbolt paused to blow smoke. "I then raised a point that had been on my mind since Mr Weatherspoon had been my client. I reminded him that he hadn't made a will. He said he had no relations and didn't care a damn about making a will. I stressed that if one of my clients, worth half a million dollars, dies, not making a will, it could cause a lot of legal problems. He sat where you are sitting, staring at me, then he gave me an odd smile. I think I can describe it was more of a cynical smirk than a smile." Benbolt fussed with his cigar, carefully knocking off ash into his oynx ash-bowl. "He said he hadn't thought of that. Then he said he wanted all his money and the grocery store to be left to a Miss Peggy Wyatt of Searle."

I kept my face expressionless.

"Did he give any reason for this?" I asked.

"I asked who Miss Wyatt was. He said she had been his mistress and he had treated her badly. He had no one else to leave his money to, so why not her? He gave this cynical smirk again and said she wouldn't get it anyway as he had no intentions of dying, but, if he did, he wanted her to get the lot. I drew up the will while he waited, and my clerks witnessed his signature." Benbolt stubbed out his cigar. "So Miss Wyatt will inherit at least half a million dollars."

"Does she know?"

"Mr Weatherspoon only died yesterday. The will has to be proved. I propose to go to Searle sometime next week and tell her."

"And the frog factory? If someone buys it, I take it the proceeds go to Weatherspoon's estate and Miss Wyatt will get the money?"

"I imagine so." Benbolt looked doubtful. "Mr Weatherspoon took from me all the documents relating to the factory. If the factory is sold, I will certainly claim for Miss Wyatt."

"So, if Weatherspoon has already sold the factory, you wouldn't know?"

"That is so, but, as soon as the will has been proved, I intend to visit the factory and find out what is happening."

"The factory won't remain unsold for long. Keep tabs on it, Mr Benbolt. You tell me Weatherspoon took all the documents referring to the factory so where are they?"

"That I don't know. I could ask his bank."

"Would you do that? Would you let me know?"

"I suppose I could." He took another cigar from the box, stared at it, then put it back. "You really mean that Mr Weatherspoon was dealing in drugs?"

"Yes, and the factory was the lynch-pin, and the racket was so profitable, I am sure the next owner will carry on."

163

He rubbed his double chin.

"Shouldn't you consult the police, Mr Wallace?"

"I'm going to, then they'll come breathing down your neck. Just get your end of it ready for inspection as I'm trying to get my end ready." I got to my feet. "The Drug Enforcement people can get very tough."

"I can only tell them what I've told you," he said, looking uneasy.

"You are now representing Miss Wyatt. Someone will buy the frog factory before long. You are in a better position to find out who the buyer is than I am. The buyer will be another drug pusher. You find out who he is and the Drug Enforcement people will love you. Inquire around and let me know who buys the factory. Will you do that?"

"I think we should talk to the police about this."

"Not yet. I want to tie this up myself. Colonel Parnell has a full report of what is happening. He'll be back from Washington in five days. Play along with me, Mr Benbolt. Just find out who buys the factory."

He thought about this, then nodded.

"Well, the will's not proved yet. I'll make inquiries. Where can I contact you?"

I gave him my business card.

"Just leave a message and I'll be with you. This is a big one, Mr Benbolt. Don't let us make a balls of it. I have still to get proof. You call in the cops now and they could trample over what I have done and come up with nothing. Okay?"

"I'll see what I can find out."

We shook hands and I left him.

I returned to my office, sat down and turned over in my mind what I had learned.

It seemed to me that Weatherspoon had got sudden cold feet. He was about to run, plus his money, now converted into cash. He had gone to old Jackson's cabin and had searched with an axe. He was after Jackson's stash of money. Maybe he had found it. While searching, someone had arrived, sneaked up on him and clouted him. Whoever it was had dragged his body to the frog pond. It was the usual method of disposing of drug pushers who wanted out.

I pulled my typewriter towards me and hammered out the latest developments for the colonel. He was getting quite a document. As I was putting the report in an envelope for Glenda, Terry O'Brien came in.

"Man! Was I lucky!" he exclaimed, dropping into a chair. "I went to Bernie Isaacs who runs an agency for strippers. Just dead luck! He acted for a stripper who called herself Stella Costa."

"Nice, quick work, Terry." I lifted my feet onto the desk. "So ...?"

O'Brien flicked an envelope across my desk.

"There she is."

I took the half-plate glossy from the envelope. Stella Costa had on only a G-string. She was certainly a sex symbol. She was posed, her legs apart, her hands above her head, her face lit with sensual excitement. I took time, studying her, then dropping the photograph on my desk, I looked at O'Brien.

"What else, Terry?"

"This costed, Dirk. The fink asked a hundred, but I beat him down to fifty."

I thought of Glenda. She would go out of her skull when I put in my expense account.

"What did he tell you?"

"For fifty, he gave me the photograph, but the sonofabitch then clammed up. I had to give him another fifty to get him talking."

I groaned.

"Well, you know how it is, Dirk. In this racket you have to pay from time to time."

"What did he come up with?"

"This stripper came to him when she was a kid. He thought around eighteen. She had no experience, but he took a fancy to her. I guess she did a casting-couch job on him. He got her small jobs in the various sleazy nightspots. She learned her trade the hard way. She worked for him for the next ten years, by then she really knew her business. Bernie's best client was Edmundo Raiz who owns the Skin Club. He got her in there. This was a big jump up for her, according to Bernie. She worked for Raiz for the next eight or nine years, then a year ago, she came to Bernie and told him she was quitting. Bernie went along with that. By then, she was pushing forty and putting on weight. She just took off and he hasn't seen nor heard of her since."

"Bernie didn't mention she had a child?"

"Oh, sure. He said the child was a handicap. She wouldn't do afternoon shows because she had to look after her boy. Bernie went along with that. He has ten children of his own, but he said without the child she could have made a lot more money."

I pushed the photograph towards him.

"Take a close look at this woman. Never mind her tits. Concentrate on her face."

He studied the photograph, then gave me a leer.

"Hard not to concentrate on her tits, isn't it?"

"If you can, throw what you call your mind back to those wedding photos of Mr and Mrs Herbert Stobart Fan showed you. Do you see a resemblance between Mrs Stobart and Stella Costa?"

He gaped at me, then studied the photograph again.

166

"Well, maybe. Yes, damn it, it's possible. You mean this stripper is Mrs Stobart?"

"I don't know. Is she?"

"I wouldn't swear to it, but the likeness is remarkable now you point it out."

I looked at my watch. The time was 18.08.

"I've another job for you, Terry. Have dinner, then do a tour of the drag clubs in Secomb. Go first to Flossie Atkins' joint. He's been in the business now for years. If you draw blank there, try all the other clubs. I want you to ask if anyone knows, has met, has seen recently, a fair-haired boy in way-out gear, beads and bracelets, going around with a big coloured man. The boy calls himself Johnny Jackson. His father was a Medal of Honor hero. The boy could have boasted about this. Okay?"

O'Brien grimaced.

"If you say so. That's a job I could well do without."

"That's the way the cookie crumbles. Don't spend any more money. Pass the word that Johnny Jackson has come into money and you want to find him."

"Flossie Atkins first, huh?"

"You could strike gold there. Keep at it, Terry. Work all night if you have to. As soon as you have some solid information, telephone me."

"I take it you'll be happily in bed."

"Could be. Phone me at my place."

"Okay," and he left.

After some thought, I decided it was now time for me to take a long look at Mrs Phyllis Stobart.

Having returned to my apartment, taken a shower, changed into one of my better suits, I drove to a seafood restaurant and fortified myself with king-sized prawns served in a green pepper sauce. I took my time. When the hands of my watch showed 19.30, I got in my car and drove to Broadhurst Boulevard.

The Stobart residence was situated at the top end of the boulevard on a corner site. All the villas on the boulevard were lush and reeked of wealth. The Stobart residence was no exception. It was half concealed by high box hedges and had double wrought-iron gates that led to a short drive past flowerbeds, immaculate lawns, a big swimming pool and all the other gimmicks the rich can't live without.

I parked under the shade of trees, got out of the car and wandered to the gates. From there I had a good view of the villa: two storeys, having probably six bedrooms, three garages and a living-room with big picture-windows stretching the entire length of the villa. In that room, one could entertain some hundred people without feeling crushed.

The front door, oak and nail-studded, was lit by two carriage lanterns. Lights were on in the living-room. Lights were also on in two of the upper bedrooms. A cream and brown Rolls stood on the tarmac. As I watched, a shadow crossed one of the upper windows: a woman.

A hard, cop voice said behind me, "What do you think you're up to?"

If someone had goosed me with a hot iron, I couldn't have jumped higher. Cautiously, I turned my head. In the hard, white light of the moon, I saw a big thickset man, wearing a peaked cap, the moonlight glittering on his silver buttons. He had a gun in his hand and was standing a foot or so behind me.

With relief, I recognized the uniform and the man. He was Jay Wilbur of the Alert Security guards with whom we often worked. They had the thankless task of patrolling the districts where the rich resided.

"Jesus, Jay!" I exclaimed. "You nearly made me lay an egg!" He peered at me, then put away his gun and grinned.

"Oh, you. What's going on?"

"I'm taking a look at the Stobart set up. Nice, huh?"

"You can say that. What's with it with the Stobarts?"

"We are interested in Mrs Stobart. I want to talk to her."

"What's the interest?"

I gave him a long, hard stare.

"Do you want to know?"

As he always received a Christmas turkey from the colonel and a bottle of Scotch at Thanksgiving, he widened his grin.

"I guess not."

"You know the lady?"

"I've seen her often enough. She's snooty. I wouldn't want to know her."

"I want to talk to her without her husband. Any ideas?"

"As regular as clockwork, she'll leave with him in half an hour to go to the Country Club. Mr Stobart drops her there and goes on to a poker club. He spends most of the night making or losing money. He picks her up at the club around one o'clock, then bed."

"Sounds as if they didn't get along together."

"You haven't seen him? No one could get along with Herbie Stobart. He's the original sonofabitch."

"Who else lives up there, Jay?"

"They have a biggish staff. There's a black buck who drives Stobart: a bodyguard type. Then there's a girl who drops in from time to time and borrows Mrs Stobart's car."

"Who is she?"

"I wouldn't know. She looks sexy: black hair, good tits. She and Mrs Stobart seem friends."

"Okay, Jay, and thanks." Knowing him, I produced a twenty-dollar bill which changed ownership as we shook hands.

All operators of the Parnell Detective Agency were members of the Country Club, the Yacht Club, the Casino and all the lush nightclubs. All operators carried the Parnell credit card which entitled them free meals, free drinks, you-name-it-you-have-it in all these clubs. It must have cost Parnell a bomb, but it paid off. There was always Charles Edwards, our accountant, to check any excessive spending and you had to have a watertight explanation when your expense sheet was checked every month.

I was installed in a lounging-chair on the big terrace of the club, nursing a Scotch and soda when I saw the cream and brown Rolls pull up at the entrance. A woman slid out, waved and came up the steps. I had hoped to have had a look at Herbert Stobart, but the Rolls drove away before I could get to my feet.

The woman was elegantly dressed in a black and white low cut gown. Diamonds glittered around her neck and wrists. Her blonde hair was swept up in a knot on the top of her head.

She moved leisurely as if she had all the time in the world. She looked around and waved to a fat man and a fatter woman who were nibbling at cocktails. They gave her a languid wave back. She went into the lobby. Hastily finishing my drink, I followed her in.

She was talking to Johnson, the club's porter, an ageing black man with white frizzy hair who was listening respectfully. Then she gave him a curt nod and went through the main lounge and out onto the rear terrace where dinner was being served. She looked around as if hoping to find someone she knew, but the big crowd was busy eating and talking as if they all were stone-deaf. She gave a little shrug and walked down to the lower terrace, found a table and sat down. She flicked impatiently at a waiter, spoke to him, then, opening her handbag, she took out a solid gold cigarette case and selected a cigarette. Her movements were slow as if she had in mind the night ahead of her would be long. She lit the cigarette, then leaned back and surveyed the moonlit sea, the rustling palms and the headlights of the passing cars, a bored expression on her face.

I moved closer. Regarding her, I could see, at one time, she must have been sensationally beautiful. She had the right bone structure, but now her face was a little puffy from too many pre-lunch cocktails and too many after-dinner Scotches. I had no doubt that this woman I was regarding was Stella Costa, ex-stripper and ex-hooker.

I hung around until the waiter served her a dry martini, then, seeing no one was showing any interest in her, I decided to try my luck.

"It's Mrs Stobart?" I said as I reached her table.

She looked sharply at, me, then she smiled. Her hard face changed with the smile.

"I am Mrs Stobart, and who are you?" She had a low, husky voice that oozed sex.

"Dirk Wallace," I said. "Lovely women should never be on their own. Would it ruin your evening if I joined you or shall I fade away?"

Again she regarded me, then her smile widened.

"Don't do that. Everyone seems paired off this evening. I come here regularly. I don't remember seeing you before."

I pulled up a chair and sat down, signalling to the waiter.

"I look in from time to time. Business keeps me busy." I ordered a Scotch on the rocks as the waiter came up.

"Busy? Even in the evening?" She looked quizzically at me.

"Yes, unfortunately." I gave her my wide, friendly smile. "Quite a crowd here."

She shrugged.

"There always is." She eyed me thoughtfully. "What is your business, Mr Wallace?"

"I am an investigator."

Her smile slipped slightly.

"How interesting! An investigator? What do you investigate?"

"Oh, this and that: confidential work."

The waiter brought my drink and I signed for it.

By her slowly changing expression I saw that she was beginning to regret inviting me to join her. She looked around as if hoping to see someone she knew so she could get up and go, but she wasn't having any luck this evening.

"I work for the Parnell Detective Agency," I went on, watching her.

She was good, but not quite good enough. She flinched, but her hand was steady as she picked up her glass, sipped the martini, then set the glass down.

"Are you telling me you are one of those horrible insects who pry into people's lives? A snooper?" Her voice had turned harsh and she looked what she was: a hooker who had struck it rich.

"I guess that's as good a description as any." I gave her my candid smile.

"Do you mean to tell me the club's committee would allow someone like you to become a member?"

"So it seems. You know, Mrs Stobart, it's surprising the people the committee do let into this club. It seems they even let in ex-hookers." Again my candid smile.

That hit her. She looked away.

"Leave me!" she said in a strangled voice. "I don't associate with people like you!"

"My mother once warned me never to associate with hookers, Mrs Stobart," I said, "but there comes a time when business is business and we both seem to be stuck with it, don't we?"

"If you don't leave immediately, I will report you to the committee!" she snarled and she looked vicious.

"Come off it, Stella," I said. "I could report you. Let's get pally. I'm not interested in you. I'm looking for your son, Johnny Jackson."

She stared down at her clenched fists for a long moment, then her fists turned into hands. She drew in along, deep breath and, with an effort, she forced herself to relax.

"By the way," I said, wanting to keep her off-balance, "Bernie Isaacs sends his compliments."

She forced a laugh.

"So you really have been digging?"

"It's part of the job." I sipped my drink, then went on, "Where do I find your son, Mrs Stobart?"

"Why do you want to find him?"

Well, that was a step forward. At least, she wasn't denying she had a son.

"Briefly, his grandfather, Frederick Jackson, hired us to find him. Now Fred is dead, his grandson – your son – inherits his grandfather's frog farm and his money. To clear up the estate, we have to find your son."

"The frog farm's worth nothing. Old Jackson didn't have any money, so why the goddamn fuss?"

"You have been misinformed, Mrs Stobart. The frog farm is worth at least twenty thousand. Old Jackson earned some two hundred dollars a week for the past forty years. I doubt if he spent more than fifty dollars a week, if that, the way he lived, so, at a very rough guess, he had saved some three hundred thousand dollars. Johnny Jackson could inherit close on a quarter of a million, death-duties and tax taken care of."

"You're out of your mind! That dreadful old man never had money like that! So, suppose he did? Where is it? In a bank? In stocks? I don't believe it!"

"He kept it in a hole under his bed. Someone found it and took it, but that doesn't mean your son isn't entitled to it."

She thought about this, staring at the moonlit sea.

"Someone took it?" she said after a long pause. "Forget it! I can tell you who took it! Johnny took it! He was the only one who would know old Jackson kept his money in a hole. When old Jackson shot himself, Johnny helped himself. It was his money, wasn't it? Old Jackson left it to him, didn't he?"

"It's a little more complicated than that. Old Jackson didn't shoot himself. He was murdered, and I think the killer got the money."

She reacted to this as if I had slapped her face. She started back and caught her breath.

"Murdered? You're crazy! What are you saying? The verdict was suicide!"

"Unless Johnny Jackson murdered his grandfather," I said quietly, "he didn't get the money he should inherit."

"That old bastard shot himself!"

"Okay. Where do I find Johnny Jackson?"

"I don't know! I've had enough of this! Get the hell away from me!" Her voice had turned strident. Fortunately, by now, the terrace was deserted, but I saw the waiter stare at us.

"Mrs Stobart, please calm down." I put a snap in my voice. "I want to find Johnny. You say you don't know

174

where he is. Can't you give me some lead? Is it right he is homosexual and goes around with a black buck?"

She hesitated, staring away from me, her hard face set.

"Yes, he is a queer," she said finally. "He came once to me with this nigger and tried to borrow money from me. I haven't seen him since. He's probably dead. I don't know ... I don't care! He was part of my miserable past."

"Why should he be dead?"

"I don't know! I've had enough of him! I just hope he is dead!"

"You can give me no idea where I can find him?"

"Oh, God!" She clenched her fists. "Can't you forget the little fag? Who cares?"

"That's not answering my question, Mrs Stobart. Have you no idea if he is around here?"

She made the effort and pulled herself together.

"I have no idea. All I hope is that he doesn't bother me ever again." She glared at me. "Do you understand? I've been through hell! Now, I have found a rich husband. My life from what it was has changed. I'm respectable!" She leaned forward, her big eyes glittering. "I've made it! Can't you understand what that means to me? I've made it, but still this ghastly little fag haunts me!"

"Oh, sure. Was Mitch Jackson his father?"

"Don't you ever stop prying? All right, if you must know, Mitch Jackson was his father. Now, are you satisfied?"

"Did you marry Jackson?"

"That bastard wasn't the marrying kind. Let me tell you, you snooping creep, like his goddamn father, Mitch only wanted a son! So I gave him a son: a homo mess! I thought Mitch would marry me when I told him he had a son, but he didn't. He got himself killed and won a medal! How's that for a laugh?"

"Johnny ran away from you when he was around eight years old. Why did he do that?"

"You want to know? Well, find out! You called me a hooker. Use what stupid brains you have." She got to her feet. "If you upset my life, Mr Private Eye, you'll be sorry." She leaned forward, glaring at me. "I've told you what I know. If you must still search for that goddamn little fag, go ahead, but keep me out of it. Understand?"

"Thank you for your co-operation, Mrs Stobart." I got to my feet. "I hope I haven't spoilt your evening."

"A turd like you *couldn't* spoil my evening," she snarled and walked away.

I watched her climb the steps to the restaurant terrace, then wave as someone claimed her.

I lit a cigarette and wandered to the balustrade and stared down at the beach and the glittering sea. I watched the young frolicking and listened to their distant shouts: Paradise City at play.

I thought about what she had told me.

I still wasn't within grasping distance of the elusive Johnny Jackson.

Back in my apartment, I switched on the TV and watched a blonde girl screaming into a mike. She jiggled her behind, clawed at the air and screamed: *I love you! I love you! I love you!* The back-up band of four coloured youths did their best to drown her squawking voice, but didn't succeed. I tried the other channels, but got more or less the same treatment so I switched off. I wondered how Terry O'Brien was making out.

The shrill sound of my telephone bell brought me awake. Looking at my watch, I saw it was a few minutes after 03.00. I grabbed the receiver.

"I hope I woke you up," O'Brien said.

"Me? I've been sitting here waiting. What have you got?"

"Look, Dirk, would you be conning me?"

"About what?"

"Johnny Jackson."

"What are you talking about?"

"I've visited about ten drag clubs and I talked to Flossie. No one ... repeat no one ... has ever heard of Johnny Jackson and, let me tell you, Flossie knows them all. He keeps a directory. He knows who is who and who does what. No Johnny Jackson."

"No fair, pretty boy going around in beads and bracelets with a black buck?"

"You heard what I said. Johnny Jackson doesn't exist. If you don't believe me, go talk to Flossie. Can I go to bed now?"

"Sure, and thanks, Terry. Maybe he didn't visit the clubs."

"How many more times do I have to tell you?" O'Brien's voice rose in exasperation. "Flossie says there is no Johnny Jackson. All these goddamn fags, as soon as I told them this guy Jackson was coming into money, fell over themselves to help, but no one has ever heard of him. Does that satisfy you?"

"It has to, doesn't it?" I said and hung up.

8

I found two notes on my desk when I entered my office the following morning.

The first read: *Mr Anderson, deputy sheriff, Searle, asks you to call him. Urgent.*

The second read: *Mr Benbolt of Howard & Benbolt, Miami, asks you to call him.*

I had had a restless night and finally slept late. After a hasty breakfast and feeling depressed, I had gone to the office. I was depressed by Terry O'Brien's report. This presented a puzzling problem. There *had* to be a Johnny Jackson. Thinking about this as I had driven to the office, I wondered if Be-Be Mansel and Phyllis Stobart had been lying to me. Why should they? Both of them had told the same story that Johnny Jackson was a homosexual and went around with a black buck. And yet Flossie Atkins had said he knew of no such pair and, from past experience, I knew Flossie was more than reliable. What possible reason could Be-Be Mansel and Phyllis Stobart have to lie to me? The evidence was there. Johnny was an obvious homosexual from what I had learned. All my informants in Searle had said he was 'soft' and didn't dig girls. If that didn't make him gay, what did?

Chick Barley was out so I had the office to myself. I put a call through to Bill Anderson.

"Dirk, I've got something for you," he said when he came on the line. He sounded efficient and excited.

"What is it?"

"I've traced the Beretta gun that killed old Jackson."

"How did you do that?"

"Well, as usual, I had nothing to do and I kept wondering about the gun so I called every cop house up the coast. I struck lucky at Jacksonville. They told me they had issued a licence for the gun six years ago."

"Who to?"

"Here's a surprise. Harry Weatherspoon."

"Nice work, Bill."

"They told me Weatherspoon, two years ago, had reported the gun had been stolen and would they cancel his permit."

"How was it stolen?"

"According to Weatherspoon, he had a break-in at the factory. Some money and the gun were stolen. He told the Jacksonville cops that Sheriff Mason was dealing with the break-in, but he wanted the permit cancelled."

"Was there a break-in, Bill?"

"No. I would have known about it. No break-in."

"How come Weatherspoon registered the gun with the Jacksonville cops?"

"I asked that. They told me he had rented an apartment there while he was looking around. He said he wanted the gun as protection. He explained to the cops that he was an ex-narcotic agent with plenty of enemies. They accepted that."

"You've done a great job, Bill! This will do you a lot of good with the colonel!"

"That's great! Do you think Weatherspoon murdered old Jackson?"

"That's my bet."

"But why for God's sake?"

"I'm working on it. When's Weatherspoon's inquest?"

"Today. The funeral will be the day after tomorrow."

"Dr Steed is sticking to the accident death?"

"Sure." He breathed heavily over the line. "Isn't it?"

I ignored this.

"About the gun, Bill. Has Dr Steed still got it?"

"I guess so. I don't know."

"Was it checked for fingerprints?"

"I wanted to do that but Dr Steed said it wasn't necessary."

"Do you even know if it was the gun that killed old Jackson?"

"There was no ballistic check if that's what you mean."

"Man! What a fig-leaf job! Okay, Bill, I'll be seeing you," and I hung up.

I then called the offices of Howard & Benbolt. I got the fat old party who, as soon as I told her my name, turned snooty.

"Mr Benbolt is out." Her voice rang with triumph.

"He asked me to call him," I said patiently, reminding myself to be kind to the old.

"I have a note here. He would like to see you this afternoon at three o'clock."

"I'll be there," I said and hung up.

I got out the carbon copies of my report to the colonel that Glenda was holding and read through them. Then I added my telephone conversation with Anderson. I sat for a little while thinking. More jigsaw puzzle pieces were falling into place. Weatherspoon decided to pull out of the drug racket, knowing old Jackson had a hidden hoard of money, had gone to the cabin and murdered old Jackson but someone had already got old Jackson's hoard. I did some more thinking. I had interviewed all the various people connected directly or indirectly with Johnny Jackson, except one: Herbert Stobart. Maybe he had never

180

heard of Johnny Jackson, but I had a strong urge to take a long look at Stobart. I had nothing to do until my date with Benbolt, so I went along to Glenda's office and gave her the report of Anderson's telephone call, asking her to keep it along with the rest of the stuff she was holding.

"Are you writing a novel?" she asked sarcastically.

"It's an idea," I grinned at her. "I hadn't thought of it, but it's an idea," and I left her.

I drove to the Country Club, parked the car and climbed the steps to the lobby. The time was 11.10. The rich and the idle were already on the terrace: the women yakking together, the men nibbling at their first drinks of the day and talking cars, sport, the Dow Jones and their money.

I found Sammy Johnson, the porter, sorting letters. He gave me a kindly smile. Colonel Parnell also looked after him at Christmas and Thanksgiving. He was a man with an ear to the ground and worth keeping sweet.

"Hi, Sammy," I said. "You're looking younger every day."

"Well, Mr Wallace," he said, smiling. "I guess that's right. I feel younger every day."

"Mr Stobart around?"

"He's playing golf, Mr Wallace." Johnson sorted more letters, then said, "I guess he'll be on the 17th by now."

"I haven't met him," I said. "How will I know him?"

"He always comes up to the lower terrace after his game. He's a little gentleman and wears a red and white striped baseball cap. You can't miss him."

"Thanks, Sammy."

"If you want to talk business with him, Mr Wallace, now's not the time. He's playing business golf with a gentleman, and Mr Stobart isn't easy."

"Thanks again, Sammy."

181

I went down to the lower terrace, found an isolated table, pulled the chair around so I was half screened by dwarf palms and sat down to wait.

Twenty minutes later, I saw a man, wearing a red and white baseball cap, a white T-shirt and dark blue slacks coming up the steps, talking to a short, heavily built man who I immediately recognized as Edmundo Raiz. I hurriedly shifted back my chair to conceal myself further. They came towards me and sat down three tables from where I was sitting.

Stobart sat with his back to me. Raiz sat by his side. Neither of them looked in my direction.

Stobart flicked his fingers at a waiter and called "Beer." Then leaning forward, he began to talk to Raiz.

Watching, I could see Raiz kept bobbing his head as if receiving instructions. I was frustrated that I couldn't see Stobart's face, but I waited patiently.

The waiter brought beers, Stobart signed and tipped and the waiter went away.

Then I saw Stobart take something from his hip pocket and then produced a pen. Standing up, peering over the palm leaves, I saw he was writing a cheque. He waved it in the air, then gave it to Raiz who put it in his wallet.

Raising his voice, Stobart said, "Okay, Ed. Get off, get cash and get the deal settled."

"Yes, Mr Stobart," Raiz said and hastily swallowed his beer. He stood up. "I'll call you as soon as I have news."

"Don't foul this up, Ed." The snap in Stobart's voice made Raiz flinch.

"You can leave this to me, Mr Stobart," and he hurried across the terrace and up the steps and out of sight.

I sat down and waited.

Stobart took his time drinking his beer. He sat still, drumming thick, short fingers on the table, and I could image his brain was active. Then abruptly he stood up and walked with quick strides to the steps.

I went after him, keeping well back. I still only had the back view of him.

In the lobby, he went to the news stand and bought a *Paradise City Herald*. I positioned myself near the revolving doors that led to the front terrace.

Below, I saw the cream and brown Rolls. A big, powerfully built negro in a brown uniform and a brown peaked cap stood waiting. I recognized him as the negro who had threatened me when I had left Hank Smith: the gorilla. Startled, I stepped back and cannoned into Stobart who was heading for the exit.

"You drunk?" he snarled, glaring at me.

We looked straight at each other and I felt a shock run through me.

I looked at this man's face confronting me: close-set eyes, an almost lipless mouth, a short nose and a thin white scar running from his right eye down to his chin.

He shoved by me and walked down the steps. The gorilla held the door open and Stobart got in. The Rolls drove away.

I watched the car out of sight. I knew for sure this man who called himself Herbert Stobart was Mitch Jackson's thieving buddy. The man who stood on the sidelines, in the past, while Mitch Jackson fought battles: the man who the citizens of Searle had said was the brains while Mitch Jackson supplied the brawn: Syd Watkins!

I found Edward Benbolt sitting behind his desk, looking flushed and, as usual, overfed.

He shook hands and waved me to a chair.

"I have just returned from Searle," he said. "In view of this offer for the frog factory, I thought it was time to talk to Miss Peggy Wyatt." He gave me a roguish smile. "Nice little girl ... lucky little girl."

"What offer?" I asked.

"Ah, Mr Wallace, things have been happening. There will be no problem concerning Mr Weatherspoon's will. Probate will be through very quickly. Mr Seigler of Seigler & Seigler came to me with a handsome offer for the factory. It was an offer I had to consider in the interest of Miss Wyatt. So, this morning, I saw her and put the proposition to her and she has agreed to sell."

"What's the offer?"

He massaged his double chin.

"Handsome."

"Look, don't go professional with me," I said in my cop voice. "I told you the buyer will be a drug pusher. What's the offer?"

"You told me that," Benbolt said, his little eyes going hard, "but I have only your word for it."

"You'll have the Drug Enforcement toughies breathing down your neck. What's the offer?"

"If I have to, Mr Wallace, I will deal directly with them and not you."

"Who's the buyer?"

He leaned back in his chair, his fat, florid face looking hostile.

"Your business, Mr Wallace, is to find Johnny Jackson. Shall we leave it at that?"

I stared at him.

"Are you saying you are no longer co-operative?"

"There is no reason for me to co-operate with a private inquiry agent." He looked more hostile. "Your insinuations

184

that the frog factory handles drugs I now consider reckless and absurd. I have inspected the factory and there is absolutely no evidence that it isn't what it claims to be: a flourishing business, supplying luxury hotels with frog saddles. By delaying the sale, many hotels will be deprived and will probably look elsewhere for supplies. Also a number of skilled workers would be thrown out of work. All this because you claim, without any evidence, that this factory is connected with drugs." He looked at his watch. "Please don't bother me again. I do not wish to waste further time with you."

I got to my feet.

"How much did they pay you, Benbolt?"

His fat face turned into an ugly mask of controlled fury. "Get out of my office!"

"Man! What you finks will do for money," I said. "See you in court," and I left him.

Going down in the elevator, I decided I had to contact Peggy Wyatt fast. There was a row of call-booths in the lobby. I hunted up *The Jumping Frog* hotel's telephone number. Old Abraham answered.

"Is Miss Peggy there, Abraham?" I asked. "This is Mr Wallace."

"No, Mr Wallace, she ain't."

"Where is she?"

"I guess up at the frog factory. You heard the wonderful news? Miss Peggy owns that factory now."

"I heard. Thanks," and I hung up. I looked up Morgan & Weatherspoon, got the number, dialled, but got the out-of-order signal. Feeling suddenly uneasy, I hung up.

It would take me a good two hours driving to reach Searle from where I was. A lot could happen in two hours. I was possibly getting worked up for nothing. Since Benbolt had told Peggy that she had inherited the factory it would be normal for her to go and look at it, but, all the same, my unease was there and when I got that feeling I acted on it. I called the sheriff's office at Searle.

Bill Anderson came on the line.

"Bill, I want you to do something," I said. "I want you to go right away to the frog factory. I want you to make sure Peggy's there, and is all right."

"All right?" He sounded puzzled. "What do you mean? You've heard the news? She's an heiress! Weatherspoon ..."

"I know all that. Get over to the factory and see what she's doing. I'm calling from a call-booth. Here's the number." I read it to him. "Got it?"

"Sure, but what's all this about?"

"Get over there! Chat her up. Congratulate her, see if she's all right, then telephone me. I'll be waiting."

"Well, okay. You'll have to wait."

"I'll wait," I said. "Get on with it!"

I expected to wait at least an hour, but trained operators are used to waiting. I took a seat in the lobby near the call-booths, lit a cigarette and thought about Benbolt.

I was sure he had been got at. I was sure Seigler of Seigler & Seigler had cut him in on the frog factory sale. I should have known better than to have confided in a fat shyster like Benbolt. I should have remembered that he was Weatherspoon's client. Could he have known what was going on at the factory? I didn't think that was likely, but it was possible. No, I decided, Benbolt was the kind who couldn't refuse big money and the money offered for him to influence Peggy to sell could have been considerable. This was a three million dollar a year take. Money to oil Benbolt would be no hardship.

So I waited.

Finally, forty minutes and six cigarettes later, I heard the bell in the call-booth ringing.

I snatched up the receiver.

"Dirk?"

"Yeah. What's happening?"

"What's all the uproar about?" Anderson sounded irritated. "I walked to the factory. Peggy was there. She looked wild with excitement. I started my stuff about being pleased about her luck, but she cut me short. I'll tell you exactly what she said. 'Not now, Bill. Some other time. I'm busy completing a deal,' and she shut the door in my face."

"That all?"

"That's it. She looked happy and excited. Did you think something was wrong?"

"A deal? Someone was with her?"

"That's correct. I saw him through the office window as I went up the steps: a little guy, dark, looked like a Mexican."

"Shit!" I said and hung up.

I ran to my car.

As I approached, I saw a fair-haired boy around twelve years old, staring at the front of my car. He looked at me and gave me a wide smile.

"You gotta flat, mister," he said. "I saw the guy. He stuck a knife in your tyre."

I looked at the offside front tyre. It couldn't have been flatter.

"What did he look like?" I asked the kid.

"A spade. Big black hat. Plenty of beads and he smelt like garbage."

Sombrero!

I got the spare wheel out and began the chore of changing wheels. I hadn't changed a wheel in years and, after minutes of fumbling, the kid said, "You haven't the right idea, mister. Let me do it."

He did it in ten minutes. I couldn't have done it in half an hour.

"What's your name, son?" I asked as he put the flat in the trunk.

"Wes Bridley."

"If ever you want to be a private eye, you come to the Parnell Detective Agency and I'll see you get employed." I gave him a five-dollar bill.

"Private eye? Who wants to be that!" He screwed up his nose. "I'm going to be a banker."

I got in the car, waved to him and headed for Searle.

I kept to the coast road, driving just within the speed limit until I reached Fort Pierce, then I turned onto highway 8. The run up to Fort Pierce had been frustrating as the coast traffic was heavy and I was sure Raiz had told Sombrero to use delaying tactics, but by careful and smart driving I kept to within forty and fifty miles an hour, not wanting more delay with a traffic cop. Once on highway 8, the traffic thinned and, taking a chance, I moved up into the sixties.

My mind was busy thinking about Peggy. I thought of Stobart giving Raiz a check and telling him to get cash. Raiz, by now, had probably talked Peggy into selling the factory, dazzling her with a pile of dollar bills.

It was when I was within five miles of Lake Placid that I became aware of a truck loaded with crates of oranges within fifteen feet of my rear bumper. Then I remember the truck had been following me for sometime. There were always dozens of trucks carrying vegetables and fruit on the highway and I had thought nothing of it. But driving at sixty-three miles an hour and to find the truck so close to me brought me alert.

Ahead of me the road was straight, bordered by trees and jungle. The truck irritated me to be driving so close and well above the speed limit for commercial vehicles. I decided to lose it and trod down hard on the gas. My car surged forward to seventy-five miles an hour. A quick check in my driving-mirror showed the truck had fallen back. I had gained some hundred yards, but I couldn't keep up this speed. Oncoming trucks had appeared and, ahead of me, I saw a massive twenty-tonner, loaded with vegetables, crawling. I had to slam on my brakes and wait for a chance to overtake. As it happened the oncoming traffic thickened. Looking in my rear mirror I saw the orange-carrying truck was again within fifteen feet of me.

It was a shabby truck with Miami number plates. It had a blue-tinted windshield so I couldn't see the driver. I saw my chance to overtake and trod down hard on the gas. I had a nasty heart-skipping moment as I got back to my right side. A car travelling much too fast had rounded the slight bend and we nearly smashed into each other. I heard the complaining sound of a horn as the car vanished from sight.

I tried to relax, but warning bells were ringing in my mind and the bells became shrill as looking into my rear mirror I saw the orange-carrying truck had crept up and was again within fifteen feet of me. We were both now travelling at over seventy miles an hour. Then, for a brief moment, I saw a black arm resting on the open window of the truck.

A black man!

On my left was a deep ditch, then trees, then jungle. The ditch was there to siphon off water when the tropical rains came. I looked in the rear mirror. *The truck had disappeared!* Sweating, I looked to my right. The goddamn truck was right beside me. It was too high for me to see the driver, but I knew what he was planning to do. He was going to sideswipe me and smash me and the car into the ditch.

My instinct was to stand on the gas, but this was no ordinary truck. It could match my speed, so I trod down hard on the foot-brake, tightening my grip on the steering wheel in case my back wheels went into a skid.

My brakes were good. With a screaming of tortured tyres, I saw the truck flash by me, its rear fender just scraping my front fender. I had a struggle to keep my car from diving into the ditch, but with sheer strength I corrected the skid.

But not so the truck. The driver had been so intent on smashing into me, he must have taken his eyes off the road. His onside wheels mounted the soft grass verge and the truck began to tilt. The load of oranges shifted, then the truck smashed down into the ditch. Crates of oranges tore loose, spilling fruit all over the jungle in a golden river. The sound of tearing metal filled the air.

I stopped my car and got out. The lumbering twenty-ton truck came on the scene and stopped. The oncoming traffic also stopped. Truckers and men in business suits got out of their vehicles. Joined by them, I walked to the upturned truck. We peered into the driving cabin.

Both Sombrero and Goatskin had their heads half through the shattered windshield. They weren't a pretty sight. Apart from blood and mangled faces, all that was left of them was their smell of dirt.

The hands of the clock on my dashboard showed 18.30 as I pulled up outside *The Jumping Frog* hotel. I had had to hang around until the State police arrived to tell them I had seen the orange-carrying truck lose control and smash into the ditch. They were more interested in getting the traffic started and the mess cleared up.

"These blacks drive too fast," the cop in charge said in disgust. "These two had a reason. The truck was stolen."

That I had guessed. I told him I was in a hurry. He said I might be called as witness, but he doubted it.

Approaching Searle, I turned over in my mind what had happened. I had no doubt that an attempt had been made on my life. From now on, I told myself, I had to be much more on my guard. I wondered if Benbolt had tipped off Raiz that I knew about the drug-ring. This was possible, depending on how much he had been paid to handle the frog factory deal.

I thought with satisfaction of my report and the can of frog saddles that were waiting for the colonel's return. No matter what happened to me, the drug-ring would be smashed, but I was going to take care nothing did happen to me.

I found old Abraham behind the reception desk. He gave me a wide, happy smile.

"Where's Miss Peggy?" I asked.

"Right there in the office, Mr Wallace. She's with Mr Willis Pollack, the lawyer gentleman. You heard the great news? Miss Peggy is rich."

"Where's her father?"

He lost his smile.

"He's in bed. The poor, dear man. I guess he's not long for this life."

I moved around the reception desk, knocked on the office door and entered.

Pollack, looking more like Buffalo Bill than ever, was sitting in a lounging chair. Peggy was behind the desk. They were splitting a bottle of champagne between them.

"Hi, Dirk!" Peggy exclaimed with a wide smile of welcome. "Where have you been?" She produced a glass. "We are celebrating. Join us!"

I moved in and closed the door.

"Not for me, but thanks," I said. "What are you celebrating?"

"I've sold the frog factory! Harry left everything to me! I'm rich!"

I pulled up a chair and sat astride it.

"That's fast work. Weatherspoon isn't even buried."

"Tell him, Mr Pollack. I want him to know," Peggy said and poured champagne into the glass, and pushed it towards me across the desk. "Come on, Dirk, you're in this celebration as much as I am."

So I picked up the glass and saluted her, drank a little and set down the glass.

"Well, Mr Wallace, this is a good deal," Pollack said. "Peggy was very wise to consult me."

"As soon as this Miami lawyer, Mr Benbolt, told me about Harry's will and that he could sell the factory for me," Peggy broke in, "I rushed to Mr Pollack, and he was with me when this man, Mr Raiz, arrived."

Pollack gave me his old-fashioned smile.

"Frankly, Mr Wallace, I didn't like the look of him, but he seemed business-like. He said he wanted to buy the factory, that any delay would mean laying off the staff and the loss of the restaurant business. That made good sense to me. He offered two hundred and fifty thousand dollars for the factory. That seemed to me a good price. I pointed out that Mr Weatherspoon's will hadn't been proved. He told me his lawyers were satisfied the factory belongs to Peggy, and there would be no problem about the probate. I then pointed out that legal transfer to him wasn't possible until the will was proved, so we must wait. He said, if he had to wait until the will was proved, the factory would lose value, and I accepted that. He proposed to pay fifty thousand dollars in cash. When the will was proved, he would pay a further two hundred thousand. If Peggy accepted the deposit, he could put a man in to run the factory tomorrow, keep the staff employed and continue to supply the restaurants. This was an acceptable offer, so I advised Peggy to sign and, from tomorrow, Mr Raiz is the new owner of the factory unless Mr Weatherspoon's will is disproved, which appears unlikely." He stroked his little beard and smiled. "However, after further discussion, I persuaded Mr Raiz that the fifty thousand dollars would be non-returnable should the final deal fall through. There was a little argument about this." Again he smiled. "When someone in a deal appears overanxious for the deal to go through, the other party, with experience, knows when to turn the screw." He leaned forward and patted Peggy's hand. "So, whatever happens, this little girl has fifty thousand dollars now safe in the bank."

I was tempted to tell them that the deal would not go through. I was tempted to tell them that within days the Drug Enforcement people would be swarming all over the factory and that Raiz and Stobart would be in the slammer, but why spoil their moment of happiness?

I lifted my glass, saluted Peggy and drank.

"Marvellous."

"Isn't it? I now have enough to help Dad," she said, her eyes sparkling. "I've always longed to help him. He's going to a clinic in Miami. I'm hoping and praying they will be able to help him."

I glanced at Pollack who sadly shook his head.

"I've warned Peggy," he said. "There is no hope for poor Bob."

"I don't give a damn! He's going to the clinic!" Peggy said. "What is money for except to help those one loves?"

"And the hotel?" I asked. "Is that going to be sold?"

She shook her head.

"Not now. I've changed my mind. Dad wants me to keep the hotel running. With the money I'll get for the factory and the grocery store, I plan to modernize the hotel. Mr Pollack thinks I'm right."

"What happened at the Weatherspoon inquest?" I asked Pollack.

"That was quickly over: accidental death."

I shrugged. Dr Steed was certainly being loyal to his old, drunken friend.

"Well, Peggy, congratulations again. I wish you the best of luck," and, leaving them, I went to my room. Lying on the bed, still a little shaken by the attempt on my life, I took stock.

I was on the verge of busting a drug-ring, but that hadn't been my assignment which was to find Johnny Jackson. So, following my father's advice: *When you are stuck, son, go back to square A, and you might, if you use your brains, find an important lead you have overlooked.* So I went back to square A and did some heavy thinking.

I dismissed the drug-ring, Raiz, Stobart and Stella. They were diversions. I concentrated on Wally Watkins, the kindly old man who grew roses. I saw him clearly in my mind when I had asked him if he had seen Johnny Jackson recently and recalled his hesitation – the hesitation of a good, honest man about to tell a lie.

I swung my legs off the bed and stood up. The time now was 19.20. I was hungry so I went down to the restaurant, nodded to the various salesmen who were eating and working and ordered the special: a T-bone steak.

After eating, I left the hotel, got in my car and headed towards Wally Watkins' little home.

The sun had set and the shadows were lengthening. I turned off the highway and within a couple of hundred yards of Watkins' home I parked the car off the road and walked the rest of the way. Turning the slight bend, I saw the little house. Lights showed in the living-room. The curtains were drawn. I could smell the roses.

Moving silently, I skirted the house and got around to the back. The bedrooms were in darkness. I had brought with me my powerful flashlight. I paused to listen. Only the sound of the trucks roaring along the highway came to me.

I found a little gate that led me into the back garden. I walked by the long-stemmed roses, those that had been cut to lie on Frederick Jackson's grave, and I reached the house. I could hear a voice from the TV set. The bedroom windows faced me. One of them was wide open. I threw the beam of my flashlight into the room which belonged to Wally Watkins: a thoroughly male room with a double bed, closets, no frills. I moved to the next window and sent the beam of my flashlight through the glass. This was a smaller room, a single bed, a feminine room. There was a small dressing table on which stood a bottle of perfume and things women use. What caught my attention was a wig of long blond hair on a head-stand, its tresses finely combed and dropping nearly to the floor.

I tried the window but it was locked, so I moved back to the open window, climbed silently into Wally Watkins' bedroom, opened the door carefully and moved into the dark passage.

Wally was listening to the news. I heard the telecaster saying something about an earthquake. I moved to the second door, opened it and was in the feminine bedroom. Closing the door, I looked around, sweeping the beam of my flashlight. This was a young girl's room. There were dolls on shelves against the far wall. There was a poster of a pop-group pinned on another wall. There was a brown, well-worn-looking, cuddly bear on a chair. Swinging the beam of my flashlight around, I stiffened, seeing a wooden glassed frame above the head of the bed.

I moved forward. The frame contained a medal. I moved further forward and stared at the Medal of Honor: Mitch Jackson's medal that I was sure had hung above Frederick Jackson's bed and which was now hanging above the bed ... of who? Johnny Jackson? Was he such a raving queer that he had a woman's wig, a cuddly bear, dolls? It was possible, but I felt doubt.

Moving away from the bed, I went to the closet and opened the doors. There were a few dresses hanging there: all for a young girl: cheap dresses you can buy at any store. There was a leather jacket and a couple of pairs of Levis. On a shelf, I found two brassières and three white panties.

I again looked at the Medal of Honor, then I returned to Wally Watkins' room, slid out of the window and went around to the front of the house. I pushed open the gate and walked up to the front door. I pressed the bell. I heard the TV snap off, then there was silence. I waited a few moments; then pressed the bell again. There was another long pause, then the front door opened and Wally Watkins regarded me.

"Hello, there, Mr Watkins," I said. "Dirk Wallace."

"Yes," he said, standing squarely in the doorway. "I'm afraid, Mr Wallace, your visit isn't convenient. Perhaps tomorrow?"

"Sorry, but not tomorrow. I have to talk to you about your son."

I saw him stiffen. The light from the passage was behind him and his face was in shadow.

"Mr Wallace," he said, hesitation in his voice, "I think I told you my son no longer interests me. If you have something to tell me, then it can wait until tomorrow. You must excuse me," and he began to shut the door.

I moved forward.

"Still sorry, Mr Watkins, but this is a police matter. It is just possible you could be involved. We had better talk."

"Police matter?" He gave ground and I moved into the passage and shut the front door.

"That's right," I said. "I'm still sorry, but we have to talk."

He hesitated, then lifted his shoulders in a defeated shrug. He opened the living-room door.

"Then you had better come in, Mr Wallace."

I followed him into the comfortable, neat living-room. The table was set for dinner: two places laid.

"I hope this won't take long, Mr Wallace," he said. "I was about to have dinner." He hesitated, then his old-world courtesy forced him to ask, "Perhaps I can offer you a drink?"

"Thanks, no." I went to a lounging-chair and sat down. "I'm sorry to tell you your son is in serious trouble. In a few days he will be arrested. He has been running a drug-ring right here in Searle." I was watching the old man and saw him flinch.

"My son? Here? In Searle?" He moved to a chair and dropped heavily into it. "I don't understand. Syd here?"

"Not in Searle. He has been living in Paradise City under the name of Herbert Stobart. He has a house worth at least half a million dollars and a Rolls Royce. He and Harry Weatherspoon organized a very profitable drug-ring. The yearly take is over three million dollars."

"Weatherspoon?" The old man looked utterly dazed.

"Let me explain, Mr Watkins. Most of what I am going to tell you is based on guess work, but I have strong evidence that my guesses are correct. It began in Vietnam. Weatherspoon was a narcotic agent, working with the Army. The drug situation in the Army was bad. Weatherspoon found out who was supplying drugs to the kids, serving in the Army. This drug pusher had to have a contact to supply the drugs. Weatherspoon found out the contact was your son. Before the drug-pusher, Mitch Jackson, could be arrested, he was killed in battle. Weatherspoon must have discovered how much money was passing hands. He was a man greedy for money, so he contacted your son and they did a deal. When they were demobilized, between them, they dreamed up an idea of using canned frogs to supply rich degenerates with heroin. The drug was in sachets, supposed to be a sauce to go with the frog saddles. It was a nice idea and a safe one. Your son developed an impressive mail order list of names, sent heroin in the cans of frog saddles to these people once a month. Weatherspoon handled the canning end and your son handled the customers and supplied the heroin. Then something happened. I don't know what, but Weatherspoon decided to pull out. He had made half a million, so he decided to quit. Maybe he quarrelled with your son. I don't know. It doesn't matter. Like most drug-traffickers who decide to get out of the racket, he ended up dead. The frog factory has just been bought by a Mexican,

Edmundo Raiz, financed by your son. These two imagine they can continue their racket, but I have enough evidence to put them away for some fifteen years."

Watkins sat motionless for some moments, then he looked at me.

"I have told you I want nothing to do with my son. What you tell me is shocking, and I hope Syd gets what he deserves. I suppose I should thank you for telling me this, but I can't see it is any concern of mine. It is hurtful, of course, but Syd has always hurt Kitty and myself. You said something about me being involved." He looked directly at me. "Am I involved?"

I ignored this, wanting to keep him off balance.

"It's odd the way things happen, Mr Watkins," I said. "Some ten days ago, the Agency received a request from the late Frederick Jackson to find his grandson. As Jackson sent us one hundred dollars as a retainer, we accepted the assignment, but only because Jackson reminded Colonel Parnell that his son, Mitch, who served in Vietnam under Parnell, had won the Medal of Honor. I got the job to find Johnny Jackson. While making inquiries, I uncovered this drug-ring. This happens to be a side issue, although an important one. I still haven't found Johnny Jackson. I asked you the other day if you had seen him recently, and you said you hadn't. I was under the impression then, and I am more sure now, you were not telling me the truth. So I ask you again: have you seen Johnny Jackson recently?"

He stared down at his hands and said nothing.

"Have you seen Johnny Jackson recently?" I repeated.

I saw by the pained expression on his face he was steeling himself to tell another lie, but at this moment, the door jerked open and Be-Be Mansel came in.

"Okay, you creep, on your way!" she snapped. "On your feet and beat it!"

I regarded her. She was wearing a T-shirt that emphasized her small rounded breasts, and tight Levis. Her long black hair was silky and reached nearly to her waist. Her small white face was as hard as stone.

"Sure," I said and stood up. I looked at Watkins, still sitting staring down at his hands. "Mr Watkins, you haven't answered my question."

Be-Be rushed up to me, grabbed my arm and swung me around.

"Get out!" she screamed at me.

I looked down at her, then the whole set-up jelled in my mind: the second bedroom, the cuddly bear, the clothes in the closet and the Medal of Honor on the wall. "Okay," I said. "I'm on my way."

She went to the door and threw it wide open.

"Get out of here!"

As I moved by her, I caught hold of a handful of her silky black tresses and jerked the wig off her head. She screamed, then her hand lashed out, but I caught her wrist.

I stared at her blonde, boyish haircut. She looked like a replica of the late Jean Sebourg.

I smiled at her.

"Hello, Johnny Jackson," I said. "So I've found you at last."

The hum of heavy trucks on the distant highway was the only sound in the neat, comfortable living-room.

Wally Watkins sat as if turned to stone. The girl was also motionless. She looked at me, then at him.

I let the silence hang, then Watkins said gently, "I think, Johnny dear, we should give Mr Wallace an explanation."

"Oh, go ahead!" she exclaimed, grabbing the wig out of my hand. "Tell him!" And she ran out of the room, slamming the door behind her.

Watkins regarded me.

"Perhaps you will join me in a little Scotch, Mr Wallace? Perhaps you would be so kind as to fix the drinks. My knee is playing up."

"Sure, but what about your dinner?" I went to the liquor cabinet and poured two drinks. "I'm sorry about this, Mr Watkins."

"Oh, dinner can wait. It is nothing grand." He took the glass, eyed the colour of the Scotch and nodded. "You make a good drink, Mr Wallace."

I carried my glass to the armchair and sat down.

"You don't have to tell me anything, Mr Watkins. I have found Johnny Jackson and that ends my assignment," I said.

"I wish it were as simple as that," he said and sipped his drink. "I want you to hear the story of Johnny Jackson, then I hope you will be more understanding towards her."

I lit a cigarette and relaxed back in the chair.

"Okay. So tell me."

"I will be as brief as I can. Both Kitty and I have been in on this sad story from the beginning. We were disappointed with our son. I don't have to go over that again. We love children. When Johnny first came to Searle and came to our store, we both took a great interest in her. We both thought she was a boy. We knew how old Fred lived and we asked Johnny if he would like to have a weekly bath at our place. Old Fred never took a bath. In fact, there was no bath at his cabin. Johnny loved that. So we saw him regularly, and we grew to love him. Mr Wallace, I now regard Johnny as my own daughter. It was when Johnny reached the age of fourteen that Kitty suspected he wasn't a boy, but a girl. By then, Johnny loved us, but not as much as she loved that dirty, rough old man. One evening when she was here for her bath, she confided in us." Watkins paused to sip his drink, then went on, "His mother Stella Costa met Mitch Jackson just before he was drafted. There was something about Mitch that fascinated women. Stella became pregnant with Johnny. She begged Mitch to marry her and he told her, providing the child was a boy, he would marry her on his return from Vietnam. This woman longed to marry Mitch. It's something I don't pretend to understand. So when the baby was born and was a girl, Stella realized Mitch now wouldn't marry her. In desperation, she registered the baby's birth as Johnny Jackson, a boy, and sent Mitch a copy of the certificate, reminding him that he had promised to marry her on his return. Now, it appears, the Jacksons were very odd. They were only interested in male heirs. Neither of them had time for female heirs. Mitch wrote back, delighted, and renewed his promise to marry Stella on his return. Stella brought her child up as a boy. She was having a hard time as Mitch sent her no money. She found Johnny, now eight years old, a hindrance. She decided to send him to his grandfather. She explained the sordid story to Johnny, instilling into him or her that he or she must never tell old Jackson he was a girl, and at that age Johnny liked being a boy. Old Jackson was delighted to have a grandson. In his rough way, he treated Johnny well, and Johnny came to love and admire this old man. She told us how, at nights, old Jackson would tell her tales about his life, about his alligator fights, and he would talk about Mitch. So the years passed. Then, of course, Johnny became more girl than boy. Often, old Jackson would talk about girls, and his talk was crude and brutal, and Johnny realized that if he found out she was a girl she would lose him."

Watkins looked at me. "It's sad, isn't it? By then Johnny really worshipped this old man, but she became more and more aware that soon he would realize she was a girl. By then, my Kitty was dead, but Johnny came regularly once a week for her bath, and we would talk. She was binding her chest flat to deceive old Jackson, but the tension of discovery became too much for her. I advised her to leave him and come and live with me. Rather than face his fury when he discovered the truth, she did this. Neither of us expected old Jackson to write to Colonel Parnell. Then you came investigating and you have found out the sad truth. Now you know, Mr Wallace. We have nothing to be ashamed of. It now doesn't matter because Johnny is going away. I have fixed her up with a job in Los Angeles. My nephew runs a dress-shop there and he is willing to have her. She'll be off tomorrow and I hope she will be happy." He smiled sadly. "I will miss her."

"That I can understand, Mr Watkins." I stared thoughtfully at him. "There are still a lot of loose ends. There's the money for instance."

His expression showed surprise.

"Money? What money?"

"Old Jackson's money."

"Did he have money? I know nothing about that."

I decided he was telling the truth.

"Johnny left her grandfather about two months ago," I said, "and she came to live with you. What did she do?"

"She told me she had work in Miami at some club. It wasn't my business. She only stayed with me weekends. One should never inquire too deeply in the affairs of the young, Mr Wallace."

"I guess that's right. I have to talk to Johnny, Mr Watkins. There are loose ends still to be tied up. I'm hoping she'll be frank with me, but she won't if you're around. Do you mind?"

He thought about this, then shook his head.

"I've no business to mind. I just ask you to be kind to her. She's had a rough life, Mr Wallace, and I love her."

I got to my feet.

"Let me fix you another drink. I'll try not to be long, then you two can get on with your dinner."

"Thank you."

I fixed him another drink and moved to the door.

"Be kind to her," he said again.

I went down the passage, knocked on the second bedroom door and went in. She was expecting me. She was half lying on the bed, holding the cuddly bear. She was wearing the blonde wig and her expression was sullen.

"Let's talk," I said, closing the door. I went to a chair and sat astride it. "What happened to your grandpa's money?"

She tightened her grip on the bear.

"I took it."

"Will you tell me about it, Johnny?"

She hesitated, then shrugged.

"He wanted Mitch to have it, then when Mitch was killed he wanted Mitch's son to have it, and if Mitch didn't have a son he wanted it to go to the Disabled Veterans fund."

"I know that. As you were his granddaughter you have no claim on the money."

"That's right. I took it because that bastard Weatherspoon was trying to steal it."

"Let's slow the pace, Johnny. Do you know about the drug-ring and the frog factory?"

"I knew. My mother told me."

"You knew your father, Weatherspoon and Stobart worked together?"

"My father was dead when those two creeps got together. So okay, my father was a drug pusher, but what the hell? He died saving seventeen little creeps, and he won the Medal of Honor."

I wasn't going to tell her Mitch went into that jungle to try to save his big weekly pay-off.

"What have you done with the money, Johnny?"

She stared at me, her eyes flashing.

"What do you think I did with it? Listen to me, Shamus, I loved my grandfather. He was the only one in my life who treated me like a human being! I'm not counting Wally or Kitty who have done so much for me, but Grandpa was different. I loved to sit and listen to him talk. What a man! I made him tell me over and over again about his fight with the alligator and how he lost his legs. Okay, he was a little crazy in the head. He hated women. He never told me why. He used to say, 'Johnny, we men must stick together. Women cause more trouble in this world than alligators.' He was crazy about money. He had no use for money. He saved and saved, and he put the money in a hole under his bed. 'When I have gone, Johnny,' he told me, 'you take it. I don't need it. Maybe you will need it. As my grandson, I want you to have it when I've gone.' I knew as I was his granddaughter he wouldn't want me to have it. If he knew I was a girl, he would have thrown me out. Then when the news came that Mitch had been killed this man Stobart came to see Grandpa. I was in the back room of the cabin and heard what he said." She stroked the bear, not looking at me. "He said he was Mitch's buddy. He said Mitch and he had been in business together and Mitch had said if anything happened to him his father was to get his share of the business and when his father died Mitch's son Johnny was to get the money. My grandpa said he didn't want anything, but Stobart insisted. 'Mitch and I were real buddies. A deal is a deal,' he said. 'Maybe you don't want it, but the kid will.' So every month a letter came for the next six years. Grandpa didn't know I had been listening. He didn't even bother to open the envelopes, but put them in the hole with his savings."

"Have you counted it, Johnny?"

"It was too much to count. I gave up when I got to five hundred thousand."

"And you have all this money?"

She looked at me.

"Not now. It didn't belong to me. I put it all in a box and sent it to the Disabled Veteran people in New York as an anonymous gift. That's what grandpa wanted, and that's what I did."

I regarded her in awe.

"But you could have kept all this money, Johnny."

Her eyes flashed.

"What do you think I am ... a goddamn thief?"

"Sorry. I think you are goddamn nice girl."

"Don't feed me that crap. My grandpa was the world to me. If his grandson didn't have the money, then the Disabled Veterans were to have it. I wasn't his grandson. I was his granddaughter. You would have done the same, wouldn't you?"

Would I?

"I hope so, Johnny. I really hope so."

"Have you finished? I want to get Wally his dinner."

"Not quite. Tell me about Weatherspoon."

Her eyes turned cloudy and again she stroked the bear. "What about him?"

"He murdered your grandpa."

"Yes."

"Tell me."

She hesitated, then said, "I had left Grandpa and was working at the Skin Club. My mother got me the job. I went to Wally every weekend. I used my mother's car. All the time, I thought of Grandpa. Often I would sneak up there and watch him at the frog pond. I longed to talk to him, but I knew he wouldn't want me any more. I went up there the day he was murdered. That bastard Weatherspoon was talking to him in the cabin as I came from the frog pond. He was shouting something about money, then I heard a shot." She closed her eyes and her hands tightened on the bear. "Weatherspoon came out of the cabin, a gun in his hand. He looked in a panic, then he heard your car coming up the lane. He bolted into the shrubs. I knew something awful had happened and I was scared stupid. You came and went into the cabin. Both Weatherspoon and I, in our hiding-places, watched you. When you drove away, Weatherspoon ran into the cabin and came out without the gun. He got on his motorcycle, which he had left at the back of the cabin, and went off. I went into the cabin." She shuddered. "Grandpa was dead. I took the money from the hole under the bed, my father's medal and all Grandpa's papers and I drove back to Wally. I didn't tell Wally what had happened or what I had seen. That's all. Now will you go away and let me get Wally's dinner?"

I got to my feet.

"Thanks, Johnny, I guess that about clears it up."

She got off the bed, reluctantly letting go of the bear.

"You won't worry us again, will you?"

I stared directly at her, then asked, keeping my voice low, "What did you hit him with, Johnny?"

She stiffened and her face turned white.

"I don't ... what are you saying?"

"You killed Weatherspoon," I said, still speaking in half a whisper. "When he went to the cabin in the final and desperate search for your grandfather's money, you were there. You watched him hack the place to pieces. You followed him to the frog pond and you hit him. He fell into the pond and drowned and, as he fell, he grabbed your wig. It was in his hand when they got him out."

Her knees buckled and she sat down abruptly on the bed. She reached for the bear and held it tight against her breasts.

"That's how it happened, didn't it, Johnny?"

She seemed to draw strength from the bear. Colour came back to her face, her eyes lit up. She leaned forward.

"Yes, I killed him! I'm glad! Do you hear? I'm glad! He killed my grandpa! I loved my grandpa! Do you hear? I don't give a damn what happens to me! Go ahead, tell the cops! It was the greatest moment in my life when I watched that devil drown! Get out! Call the cops!" Tears began to trickle down her face. She brushed them aside impatiently. "Go on, leave us! I'll wait here for the cops. I've had enough of running away."

"The inquest on Weatherspoon's death was held today," I said quietly. "The verdict was accidental death. That's fine with me. A man who corrupts people with drugs doesn't deserve to live. You did a good job, Johnny."

She stared at me, her eyes widening. She began to say something, then stopped.

"I wish you luck, Johnny," I said. "I hope you find a better life." I smiled at her. "You are young. Your life is ahead of you. Make a success of it and keep away from Searle."

She began sobbing, waving me away.

"Go shake your goddam tambourine some place else," she gasped out.

I left her sobbing over her cuddly bear. I didn't stop to say goodbye to Wally Watkins. I left the little house, walked to my car. I lit a cigarette and sat for some minutes, thinking.

Tomorrow, I would give Colonel Parnell my report, but it would be amended. He would turn my report over to the Drug Enforcement people who would raid the frog factory and Syd Watkins' luxury house. They would find enough evidence to put Watkins and Raiz away for a long stretch. I wondered about Stella. Her future would be bleak and at her age I wondered what would happen to her. She was tough and would probably survive.

I started the car engine.

I would tell the colonel that, although I had uncovered a drug-ring, I hadn't succeeded in finding Johnny Jackson. I would ask him if he wanted me to continue the search. Knowing the colonel, I was sure he wouldn't want to spend any more money. Exposing a drug-ring would be enough for him. He would take care that the publicity would reflect well on the Agency.

As I drove towards Searle, I realized, by covering up on Johnny Jackson, it was now my turn to hand out a fig-leaf.

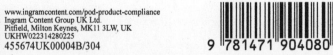